The Guild of Egg Stealers

You rob my cradle; I'll rob yours. Such was their motto, and it worked.

A Guild of Egg Stealers was formed. The Human branch of it guaranteed, for a price, to bring you a Ssassaror child to replace the one that had been stolen from you. Or, if you lived on the seashore, and an Amphibian had crept into your nursery and taken your baby—always under two years old, according to the rules—then the Guildsman would bring you an Amphib or, perhaps, the child of a Human Changeling reared by the Seafolk.

You raised it and loved it as your own. How could you help loving it?

Your Skin told you that it was small and helpless and needed you and was, despite appearances, as Human as any of your babies. Nor did you need to worry about the one that had been abducted. It was getting just as good care as you were giving this one.

It had never occurred to anyone to quit the stealing and voluntary exchange of babies. Perhaps that was because it would strain even the loving nature of the Skin-wearers to give away their own flesh and blood. But once the transfer had taken place, they could adapt.

Or perhaps the custom was kept because tradition is stronger than law in a peasant-monarchy society and also because egg-and-baby stealing gave the more naturally aggressive and daring citizens a chance to work off anti-social behavior.

RASTIGNAC THE DEVIL

PHILIP JOSÉ FARMER

WILDSIDE PRESS

RASTIGNAC THE DEVIL

Originally published in *Fantastic Universe*, May 1954.

Cover by Catmando.

Published by Wildside Press, LLC in 2010.

PROLOG

After the Apocalyptic War, the decimated remnants of the French huddled in the Loire Valley were gradually squeezed between two new and growing nations. The Colossus to the north was unfriendly and obviously intended to absorb the little New France. The Colossus to the south was friendly and offered to take the weak state into its confederation of republics as a full partner.

A number of proud and independent French citizens feared that even the latter alternative meant the eventual transmutation of their tongue, religion, and nationality into those of their southern neighbor. Seeking a way of salvation, they built six huge spaceships that would hold thirty thousand people, most of whom would be in deep freeze until they reached their destination. The six vessels then set off into interstellar space to find a planet that would be as much like Earth as possible.

That was in the 22nd Century. Over three hundred and fifty years passed before Earth heard of them again. However, we are not here concerned with the home world but with the story of a man of that pioneer group who wanted to leave the New Gaul and sail again to the stars. . . .

I

Rastignac had no Skin. He was, nevertheless, happier than he had been since the age of five.

He was as happy as a man can be who lives deep under the ground. Underground organizations are often under the ground. They are formed into cells. Cell Number One usually contains the leader of the underground.

Jean-Jacques Rastignac, chief of the Legal Underground of the Kingdom of L'Bawpfey, was literally in a cell beneath the surface of the earth. He was in jail.

For a dungeon, it wasn't bad. He had two cells. One was deep inside the building proper, built into the wall so that he could sit in it when he wanted to retreat from the sun or the rain. The adjoining cell was at the bottom of a well whose top was covered with a grille of thin steel bars. Here he spent most of his waking hours. Forced to look upwards if he wanted to see the sky or the stars, Rastignac suffered from a chronic stiff neck.

Several times during the day he had visitors. They were allowed to bend over the grille and talk down to him. A guard, one of the King's mucketeers,[1] stood by as a censor.

[1] Mucketeer is the best translation of the 26th century French noun *foutriquet*, pronounced *vfeutwikey*.

When night came, Rastignac ate the meal let down by ropes on a platform. Then another of the King's mucketeers stood by with drawn épée until he had finished eating. When the tray was pulled back up and the grille lowered and locked, the mucketeer marched off with the turnkey.

Rastignac sharpened his wit by calling a few choice insults to the night guard, then went into the cell inside the wall and lay down to take a nap. Later, he would rise and pace back and forth like a caged tiger. Now and then he would stop and look upwards, scan the stars, hunch his shoulders and resume his savage circuit of the cell. But the time would come when he would stand statue-still. Nothing moved except his head, which turned slowly.

"Some day I'll ride to the stars with you."

He said it as he watched the Six Flying Stars speed across the night sky—six glowing stars that moved in a direction opposite to the march of the other stars. Bright as Sirius seen from Earth, strung out one behind the other like jewels on a velvet string, they hurtled across the heavens.

They were the six ships on which the original Loire Valley Frenchmen had sailed out into space, seeking a home on a new planet. They had been put into an orbit around New Gaul and left there while their thirty thousand passengers had descended to the surface in chemical-fuel rockets. Mankind, once on the fair and fresh earth of the new planet, had never again ascended to re-visit the great ships.

For three hundred years the six ships had circled the planet known as New Gaul, nightly beacons and glowing reminders to Man that he was a stranger on this planet.

When the Earthmen landed on the new planet they had called the new land *Le Beau Pays*, or, as it was now pronounced, *L'Bawpfey*—The Beautiful Country. They had been delighted, entranced with the fresh new land. After the burned, war-racked Earth they had just left, it was like coming to Heaven.

They found two intelligent species living on the planet, and they found that the species lived in peace and that they had no conception of war or of poverty. And they were quite willing to receive the Terrans into their society.

Provided, that is, they became integrated, or—as they phrased it—natural. The Frenchmen from Earth had been given their choice. They were told:

"You can live with the people of the Beautiful Land on our terms—war with us, or leave to seek another planet."

The Terrans conferred. Half of them decided to stay; the other half decided to remain only long enough to mine uranium and other chemicals. Then they would voyage onwards.

But nobody from that group of Earthmen ever again stepped into the ferry-rockets and soared up to the six ion-beam ships circling about Le Beau Pays. All succumbed to the Philosophy of the Natural. Within a few generations a stranger landing upon the planet would not have known without previous information that the Terrans were not aboriginal.

He would have found three species. Two were warm-blooded egglayers who had evolved directly from reptiles without becoming mammals—the Ssassarors and the Amphibs. Somewhere in their dim past—like all happy nations, they had no history—they had set up their society and been very satisfied with it since.

It was a peaceful quiet world, largely peasant, where nobody had to scratch for a living and where a superb manipulation of biological forces ensured very long lives, no disease, and a social lubrication that left little to desire—from their viewpoint, anyway.

The government was, nominally, a monarchy. The Kings were elected by the people and were a different species than the group each ruled. Ssassaror ruled Human, and vice versa, each assisted by foster-brothers and sisters of the race over which they reigned. These were the so-called Dukes and Duchesses.

The Chamber of Deputies—*L'Syawp t' Tapfuti*—was half Human and half Ssassaror. The so-called Kings took turns presiding over the Chamber for forty day intervals. The Deputies were elected for ten-year terms by constituents who could not be deceived about their representatives' purposes because of the sensitive Skins which allowed them to determine their true feelings and worth.

In one custom alone did the ex-Terrans differ from their neighbors. This was in carrying arms. In the beginning, the Ssassaror had allowed the Men to wear their short rapiers, so they would feel safe even though in the midst of aliens.

As time went on, only the King's mucketeers—and members of the official underground—were allowed to carry épées. These men, it might be noticed, were the congenital adventurers, men who needed to swashbuckle and revel in the name of individualist.

Like the egg-stealers, they needed an institution in which they could work off anti-social steam.

From the beginning the Amphibians had been a little separate from the Ssassaror and when the Earthmen came they did not get any more neighborly. Nevertheless, they preserved excellent relations and they, too, participated in the Changeling-custom.

This Changeling-custom was another social device set up millennia ago to keep a mutual understanding between all species on the planet. It was a peculiar institution, one that the Earthmen had found hard to understand and ever more difficult to adopt. Nevertheless, once the Skins had been accepted they had changed their attitude, forgot their speculations about its origin and threw themselves into the custom of stealing babies—or eggs—from another race and raising the children as their own.

You rob my cradle; I'll rob yours. Such was their motto, and it worked.

A Guild of Egg Stealers was formed. The Human branch of it guaranteed, for a price, to bring you a Ssassaror child to replace the one that had been stolen from you. Or, if you lived on the seashore, and an Amphibian had crept into your nursery and taken your baby—always under two years old, according to the rules—then the Guildsman would bring you an Amphib or, perhaps, the child of a Human Changeling reared by the Seafolk.

You raised it and loved it as your own. How could you help loving it?

Your Skin told you that it was small and helpless and needed you and was, despite appearances, as Human as any of your babies. Nor did you need to worry about the one that had been abducted. It was getting just as good care as you were giving this one.

It had never occurred to anyone to quit the stealing and voluntary exchange of babies. Perhaps that was because it would strain even the loving nature of the Skin-wearers to give away their own flesh and blood. But once the transfer had taken place, they could adapt.

Or perhaps the custom was kept because tradition is stronger than law in a peasant-monarchy society and also because egg-and-baby stealing gave the more naturally aggressive and daring citizens a chance to work off anti-social behavior.

Nobody but a historian would have known, and there were no historians in The Beautiful Land.

Long ago the Ssassaror had discovered that if they lived meatless, they had a much easier time curbing their belligerency, obeying the Skins and remaining cooperative. So they induced the Earthmen to put a taboo on eating flesh. The only drawback to the meatless diet was that both Ssassaror and Man became as stunted in stature as they did in aggressiveness, the former so much so that they barely came to the chins of the Humans. These, in turn, would have seemed short to a Western European.

But Rastignac, an Earthman, and his good friend, Mapfarity, the Ssassaror Giant, became taboo-breakers when they were children and played together on the beach where they first ate seafood out of curiosity, then continued because they liked it. And due to their protein diet the Terran had grown well over six feet in height and the Ssassaror seemed to have touched off a rocket of expansion in his body with his protein-eating. Those Ssassarors who shared his guilt—became meat-eaters—became ostracized and eventually moved off to live by themselves. They were called Ssassaror-Giants and were pointed to as an object lesson to the young of the normal Ssassarors and Humans on the land.

If a stranger had landed shortly before Rastignac was born, however, he would have noticed that all was not as serene as it was supposed to be among the different species. The cause for the flaw in the former Eden might have puzzled him if he had not known the previous history of L'Bawfey and the fact that the situation had not changed for the worst until the introduction of Human Changelings among the Amphibians.

Then it had been that blood-drinking began among them, that Amphibians began seducing Humans to come live with them by their tales of easy immortality, and that they started the system of leaving savage little carnivores in the Human nurseries.

When the Land-dwellers protested, the Amphibs replied that these things were carried out by unnaturals or outlaws, and that the Sea-King could not be held responsible. Permission was given to Chalice those caught in such behavior.

Nevertheless, the suspicion remained that the Amphib monarch had, in accordance with age-old procedure, given his unofficial official blessing and that he was preparing even more disgusting and outrageous and unnatural moves. Through his control of the populace by the Master Skin, he would be able to do as he pleased with their minds.

It was the Skins that had made the universal peace possible on the planet of New Gaul. And it would be the custom of the Skins that would make possible the change from peace to conflict among the populace.

Through the artificial Skins that were put on all babies at birth—and which grew with them, attached to their body, feeding from their bloodstreams, their nervous systems—the Skins, controlled by a huge Master Skin that floated in a chemical vat in the palace of the rulers, fed, indoctrinated and attended day and night by a crew of the most brilliant scientists of the planet, gave the Kings complete control of the minds and emotions of the inhabitants of the planet.

Originally the rulers of New Gaul had desired only that the populace live in peace and enjoy the good things of their planet equally. But the change that had been coming gradually—the growth of conflict between the Kings of the different species for control of the whole populace—was beginning to be generally felt. Uneasiness, distrust of each other was growing among the people. Hence the legalizing of the Underground, the Philosophy of Violence by the government, an effort to control the revolt that was brewing.

Yet, the Land-dwellers had managed to take no action at all and to ignore the growing number of vicious acts.

But not all were content to drowse. One man was aroused. He was Rastignac.

They were Rastignac's hope, those Six Stars, the gods to which he prayed. When they passed quickly out of his sight he would continue his pacing, meditating for the twenty-thousandth time on a means for reaching one of those ships and using it to visit the stars. The end of his fantasies was always a curse because of the futility of such hopes. He was doomed! Mankind was doomed!

And it was all the more maddening because Man would not admit that he was through. Ended, that is, as a human being.

Man was changing into something not quite *homo sapiens*. It might be a desirable change, but it would mean the finish of his climb upwards. So it seemed to Rastignac. And he, being the man he was, had decided to do something about it even if it meant violence.

That was why he was now in the well-dungeon. He was an advocator of violence against the status quo.

II

There was another cell next to his. It was also at the bottom of a well and was separated from his by a thin wall of cement. A window had been set into it so that the prisoners could talk to each other. Rastignac did not care for the woman who had been let down into the adjoining cell, but she was somebody to talk to.

"Amphib-changelings" was the name given to those human beings who had been stolen from their cradles and raised among the non-humanoid Amphibians as their own. The girl in the adjoining cell, Lusine, was such a person. It was not her fault that she was a blood-drinking Amphib. Yet he could not help disliking her for what she had done and for the things she stood for.

She was in prison because she had been caught in the act of stealing a Man child from its cradle. This was no crime, but she had left in the cradle, under the covers, a savage and blood-thirsty little monster that had leaped up and slashed the throat of the unsuspecting baby's mother.

Her cell was lit by a cageful of glowworms. Rastignac, peering through the grille, could see her shadowy shape in the inner cell inside the wall. She rose langorously and stepped into the circle of dim orange light cast by the insects.

"*B'zhu, m'fweh,*" she greeted him.

It annoyed him that she called him her brother, and it annoyed him even more to know that she knew it. It was true that she had some excuse for thus addressing him. She did resemble him. Like him, she had straight glossy blue-black hair, thick bracket-shaped eyebrows, brown eyes, a straight nose and a prominent chin. And where his build was superbly masculine, hers was magnificently feminine.

Nevertheless, this was not her reason for so speaking to him. She knew the disgust the Land-walker had for the Amphib-changeling, and she took a perverted delight in baiting him.

He was proud that he seldom allowed her to see that she annoyed him. "*B'zhu, fam tey zafeep,*" he said. "Good evening, woman of the Amphibians."

Mockingly she said, "Have you been watching the Six Flying Stars, Jean-Jacques?"

"*Vi.* I do so every time they come over."

"Why do you eat your heart out because you cannot fly up to them and then voyage among the stars on one of them?"

He refused to give her the satisfaction of knowing his real reason. He did not want her to realize how little he thought of Mankind and its chances for surviving—as humanity—upon the face of this planet, L'Bawpfey.

"I look at them because they remind me that Man was once captain of his soul."

"Then you admit that the Land-walker is weak?"

"I think he is on the way to becoming non-human, which is to say that he is weak, yes. But what I say about Landman goes for Seaman, too. You Changelings are becoming more Amphibian every day and less Human. Through the Skins the Amphibs are gradually changing you completely. Soon you will be completely sea-people."

She laughed scornfully, exposing perfect white teeth as she did so.

"The Sea will win out against the Land. It launches itself against the shore and shakes it with the crash of its body. It eats away the rock and the dirt and absorbs it into its own self. It can't be worn away nor caught and held in a net. It is elusive and all-powerful and never-tiring."

Lusine paused for breath. He said, "That is a very pretty analogy, but it doesn't apply. You Seafolk are as much flesh and blood as we Landfolk. What hurts us hurts you."

She put a hand around one bar. The glow-light fell upon it in such a way that it showed plainly the webbing of skin between her fingers. He glanced at it with a faint repulsion under which was a counter-current of attraction. This was the hand that had, indirectly, shed blood.

She glanced at him sidewise, challenged him in trembling tones. "You are not one to throw stones, Jean-Jacques. I have heard that you eat meat."

"Fish, not meat. That is part of my Philosophy of Violence," he retorted. "I maintain that one of the reasons man is losing his power and strength is that he has so long been upon a vegetable diet. He is as cowed and submissive as the grass-eating beast of the fields."

Lusine put her face against the bars.

"That is interesting," she said. "But how did you happen to begin eating fish? I thought we Amphibs alone did that."

What Lusine had just said angered him. He had no reply.

Rastignac knew he should not be talking to a Sea-changeling. They were glib and seductive and always searching for ways to twist your thoughts. But being Rastignac, he had to talk. Moreover, it was so difficult to find anybody who would listen to his ideas that he could not resist the temptation.

"I was given fish by the Ssassaror, Mapfarity, when I was a child. We lived along the sea-shore. Mapfarity was a child, too, and we played together. Don't eat fish!' my parents said. To me that meant 'Eat it!' So, despite my distaste at the idea, and my squeamish stomach, I did eat fish. And I liked it. And as I grew to manhood I adopted the Philosophy of Violence and I continued to eat fish although I am not a Changeling."

"What did your Skin do when it detected you?" Lusine asked. Her eyes were wide and luminous with wonder and a sort of glee as if she relished the confession of his sins. Also, he knew, she was taunting him about the futility of his ideas of violence so long as he was a prisoner of the Skin.

He frowned in annoyance at the reminder of the Skin. Much thought had he given, in a weak way, to the possibility of life without the Skin.

Ashamed now of his weak resistance to the Skin, he blustered a bit in front of the teasing Amphib girl.

"Mapfarity and I discovered something that most people don't know," he answered boastfully. "We found that if you can stand the shocks your Skin gives you when you do something wrong, the Skin gets tired and quits after a while. Of course your Skin recharges itself and the next time you eat fish it shocks you again. But after very many shocks it becomes accustomed, forgets its conditioning, and leaves you alone."

Lusine laughed and said in a low conspirational tone, "So your Ssassaror pal and you adopted the Philosophy of Violence because you remained fish and meat eaters?"

"Yes, we did. When Mapfarity reached puberty he became a Giant and went off to live in a castle in the forest. But we have remained friends through our connection in the underground."

"Your parents must have suspected that you were a fish eater when you first proposed your Philosophy of Violence?" she said.

"Suspicion isn't proof," he answered. "But I shouldn't be telling you all this, Lusine. I feel it is safe for me to do so only because you will never have a chance to tell on me. You will soon be taken to Chalice and there you will stay until you have been cured."

She shivered and said, "This Chalice? What is it?"

"It is a place far to the north where both Terrans and Ssassarors send their incorrigibles. It is an extinct volcano whose steep-sided interior makes an inescapable prison. There those who have persisted in unnatural behavior are given special treatment."

"They are bled?" she asked, her eyes widening as her tongue flicked over her lips again hungrily.

"No. A special breed of Skin is given them to wear. These Skins shock them more powerfully than the ordinary ones, and the shocks are associated with the habit they are trying to cure. The shocks effect a cure. Also, these special Skins are used to detect hidden unnatural emotions. They re-condition the deviate. The result is that when the Chaliced Man is judged able to go out and take his place in society again, he is thoroughly re-conditioned. Then his regular Skin is given back to him and it has no trouble keeping him in line from then on. The Chaliced Man is a very good citizen."

"And what if a revolter doesn't become Chaliced?"

"Then he stays in Chalice until he decides to become so."

Her voice rose sharply as she said, "But if I go there, and I am not fed the diet of the Amphibs, I will grow old and die!"

"No. The government will feed you the diet you need until you are re-conditioned. Except . . ." He paused.

"Except I won't get blood," she wailed. Then, realizing she

was acting undignified before a Landman, she firmed her voice.

"The King of the Amphibians will not allow them to do this to me," she said. "When he hears of it he will demand my return. And if the King of Men refuses, my King will use violence to get me back."

Rastignac smiled and said, "I hope he does. Then perhaps my people will wake up and get rid of their Skins and make war upon your people."

"So that is what you Philosophers of Violence want, is it? Well, you will not get it. My father, the Amphib King, will not be so stupid as to declare a war."

"I suppose not," replied Rastignac. "He will send a band to rescue you. If they're caught they'll claim to be criminals and say they are *not* under the King's orders."

Lusine looked upwards to see if a guard was hanging over the well's mouth listening. Perceiving no one, she nodded and said, "You have guessed it correctly. And that is why we laugh so much at you stupid Humans. You know as well as we do what's going on, but you are afraid to tell us so. You keep clinging to the idea that your turn-the-other-cheek policy will soften us and insure peace."

"Not I," said Rastignac. "I know perfectly well there is only one solution to man's problems. That is—"

"That is Violence," she finished for him. "That is what you have been preaching. And that is why you are in this cell, waiting for trial."

"You don't understand," he said. "Men are not put into the Chalice for *proposing* new philosophies. As long as they behave naturally they may say what they wish. They may even petition the King that the new philosophy be made a law. The King passes it on to the Chamber of Deputies. They consider it and put it up to the people. If the people like it, it becomes a law. The only trouble with that procedure is that it may take ten years before the law is considered by the Chamber of Deputies."

"And in those ten years," she mocked him, "the Amphibs and the Amphibian-changelings will have won the planet."

"That is true," he said.

"The King of the Humans is a Ssassaror and the King of the Ssassaror is a Man," said Lusine. "Our King can't see any reason for changing the status quo. After all, it is the Ssassaror who are responsible for the Skins and for Man's position in the sentient society of this planet. Why should he be favorable to a policy of Violence? The Ssassarors loathe violence."

"And so you have preached Violence without waiting for it to become a law? And for that you are now in this cell?"

"Not exactly. The Ssassarors have long known that to suppress too much of Man's naturally belligerent nature only results in an explosion. So they have legalized illegality—up to a point. Thus the King officially made me the Chief of the Underground and gave me a state license to preach—but not practice—Violence. I am even allowed to advocate overthrow of the present system of government—as long as I take no action that is too productive of results.

"I am in jail now because the Minister of Ill-Will put me here. He had my Skin examined, and it was found to be 'unhealthy.' He thought I'd be better off locked up until I became 'healthy' again. But the King . . ."

III

Lusine's laughter was like the call of a silverbell bird. Whatever her unhuman appetites, she had a beautiful voice. She said, "How comical! And how do you, with your brave ideas, like being regarded as a harmless figure of fun, or as a sick man?"

"I like it as well as you would," he growled.

She gripped the bars of her window until the tendons on the back of her long thin hands stood out and the membranes between her fingers stretched like wind-blown tents. Face twisted, she spat at him, "Coward! Why don't you kill somebody and break out of this ridiculous mold—that Skin that the Ssassarors have poured you into?"

Rastignac was silent. That was a good question. Why didn't he? Killing was the logical result of his philosophy. But the Skin kept him docile. Yes, he could vaguely see that he had purposely shut his eyes to the destination towards which his ideas were slowly but inevitably traveling.

And there was another facet to the answer to her question—if he had to kill, he would not kill a Man. His philosophy was directed towards the Amphibians and the Sea-changelings.

He said, "Violence doesn't necessarily mean the shedding of blood, Lusine. My philosophy urges that we take a more vigorous action, that we overthrow some of the bio-social institutions which have imprisoned Man and stripped him of his dignity as an individual."

"Yes, I have heard that you want Man to stop wearing the Skin. That is what has horrified your people, isn't it?"

"Yes," he said. "And I understand it has had the same effect among the Amphibians."

She bridled, her brown eyes flashing in the feeble glowworms' light. "Why shouldn't it? What would we be without our Skins?"

"What, indeed?" he said, laughing derisively afterwards.

Earnestly she said, "You don't understand. We Amphibians—our Skins are not like yours. We do not wear them for the same reason you do. You are imprisoned by your Skins—they tell you how to feel, what to think. Above all, they keep you from getting ideas about non-cooperation or non-integration with Nature as a whole.

"That, to us individualistic Amphibians, is false. The purpose of our Skins is to make sure that our King's subjects understand what he wants so that we may all act as one unit and thus further the progress of the Seafolk."

The first time Rastignac had heard this statement he had howled with laughter. Now, however, knowing that she could not see the fallacy, he did not try to argue the point. The Amphibs were, in their way, as hidebound—no pun intended—as the Land-walkers.

"Look, Lusine," he said, "there are only three places where a Man may take off his Skin. One is in his own home, when he may hang it upon the halltree. Two is when he is, like us, in jail and therefore may not harm anybody. The third is when a man is King. Now you and I have been without our Skins for a week. We have gone longer without them than anybody, except the King. Tell me true, don't you feel free for the first time in your life?

"Don't you feel as if you belong to nobody but yourself, that you are accountable to no one but yourself, and that you love that feeling? And don't you dread the day we will be let out of prison and made to wear our Skins again? That day which, curiously enough, will be the very day that we will lose our freedom."

Lusine looked as if she didn't know what he was talking about.

"You'll see what I mean when we are freed and the Skins are put back upon us," he said. Immediately after, he was embarrassed. He remembered that she would go to the Chalice where one of the heavy and powerful Skins used for unnaturals would be fastened to her shoulders.

Lusine did not notice. She was considering the last but most telling point in her argument "You cannot win against us," she said, watching him narrowly for the effect of her words. "We have a weapon that is irresistible. We have immortality."

His face did not lose its imperturbability.

She continued, "And what is more, we can give immortality

to anyone who casts off his Skin and adopts ours. Don't think that your people don't know this. For instance, during the last year more than two thousand Humans living along the beaches deserted and went over to us, the Amphibs."

He was a little shocked to hear this, but he did not doubt her. He remembered the mysterious case of the schooner *Le Pauvre Pierre* which had been found drifting and crewless, and he remembered a conversation he had had with a fisherman in his home port of Marrec.

He put his hands behind his back and began pacing. Lusine continued staring at him through the bars. Despite the fact that her face was in the shadows, he could see—or feel—her smile. He had humiliated her, but she had won in the end.

Rastignac quit his limited roving and called up to the guard.

"Shoo l'footyay, kal u ay tee?"

The guard leaned over the grille. His large hat with its tall wings sticking from the peak was green in the daytime. But now, illuminated only by a far off torchlight and by a glowworm coiled around the band, it was black.

"Ah, shoo Zhaw-Zhawk W'stenyek," he said, loudly. "What time is it? What do you care what time it is?" And he concluded with the stock phrase of the jailer, unchanged through millenia and over light-years. "You're not going any place, are you?"

Rastignac threw his head back to howl at the guard but stopped to wince at the sudden pain in his neck. After uttering, *"Sek Ploo!"* and *"S'pweestee!"* both of which were close enough to the old Terran French so that a language specialist might have recognized them, he said, more calmly, "If you would let me out on the ground, *monsieur le foutriquet*, and give me a good épée, I would show you where I am going. Or, at least, where my sword is going. I am thinking of a nice sheath for it."

Tonight he had a special reason for keeping the attention of the King's mucketeer directed towards himself. So, when the guard grew tired of returning insults—mainly because his limited imagination could invent no new ones—Rastignac began telling jokes. They were broad and aimed at the mucketeer's narrow intellect.

"Then," said Rastignac, "there was the itinerant salesman

whose *s'fel* threw a shoe. He knocked on the door of the hut of the nearest peasant and said . . ." What was said by the salesman was never known.

A strangled gasp had come from above.

IV

Rastignac saw something enormous blot out the smaller shadow of the guard. Then both figures disappeared. A moment later a silhouette cut across the lines of the grille. Unoiled hinges screeched; the bars lifted. A rope uncoiled from above to fall at Rastignac's feet. He seized it and felt himself being drawn powerfully upwards.

When he came over the edge of the well, he saw that his rescuer was a giant Ssassaror. The light from the glowworm on the guard's hat lit up feebly his face, which was orthagnathous and had quite humanoid eyes and lips. Large canine teeth stuck out from the mouth, and its huge ears were tipped with feathery tufts. The forehead down to the eyebrows looked as if it needed a shave, but Rastignac knew that more light would show the blue-black shade came from many small feathers, not stubbled hair.

"Mapfarity!" Rastignac said. "It's good to see you after all these years!"

The Ssassaror giant put his hand on his friend's shoulder. Clenched, it was almost as big as Rastignac's head. He spoke with a voice like a lion coughing at the bottom of a deep well.

"It is good to see you again, my friend."

"What are you doing here?" said Rastignac, tears running down his face as he stroked the great fingers on his shoulder.

Mapfarity's huge ears quivered like the wings of a bat tied to a rock and unable to fly off. The tufts of feathers at their ends grew stiff and suddenly crackled with tiny sparks.

The electrical display was his equivalent of the human's weeping. Both creatures discharged emotion; their bodies chose different avenues and manifestations. Nevertheless, the sight of the other's joy affected each deeply.

"I have come to rescue you," said Mapfarity. "I caught Archambaud here,"—he indicated the other man—"stealing eggs from my golden goose. And . . ."

Raoul Archambaud—pronounced Wawl Shebvo—interrupted excitedly, "I showed him my license to steal eggs from Giants who were raising counterfeit geese, but he was going to lock me up anyway. He was going to take my Skin off and feed me on meat. . . ."

"Meat!" said Rastignac, astonished and revolted despite himself. "Mapfarity, what have you been doing in that castle of yours?"

Mapfarity lowered his voice to match the distant roar of a cataract. "I haven't been very active these last few years," he said, "because I am so big that it hurts my feet if I walk very much. So I've had much time to think. And I, being logical, decided that the next step after eating fish was eating meat. It couldn't make me any larger. So, I ate meat. And while doing so, I came to the same conclusion that you, apparently, have done independently. That is, the Philosophy of . . ."

"Of Violence," interrupted Archambaud. "Ah, Jean-Jacques, there must be some mystic bond that brings two Humans of such different backgrounds as yours and the Ssassaror together, giving you both the same philosophy. When I explained what you had been doing and that you were in jail because you had advocated getting rid of the Skins, Mapfarity petitioned . . ."

"The King to make an official jail-break," said Mapfarity with an impatient glance at the rolypoly egg-stealer. "And . . ."

"The King agreed," broke in Archambaud, "provided Mapfarity would turn in his counterfeit goose and provided you would agree to say no more about abandoning Skins, but . . ."

The Giant's basso profundo-redundo pushed the egg-stealer's high pitch aside. "If this squeaker will quit interrupting, perhaps we can get on with the rescue. We'll talk later, if you don't mind."

At that moment Lusine's voice floated up from the bottom of her cell. "Jean-Jacques, my love, my brave, my own, would you abandon me to the Chalice? Please take me with you! You will need somebody to hide you when the Minister of Ill-Will sends his mucketeers after you. I can hide you where no one will ever find you." Her voice was mocking, but there was an undercurrent of anxiety to it.

Mapfarity muttered, "She will hide us, yes, at the bottom of a sea-cave where we will eat strange food and suffer a change. Never . . ."

"Trust an Amphib," finished Archambaud for him.

Mapfarity forgot to whisper. "*Bey-t'cul, vu nu fez yey! Fe'm sa!*" he roared.

A shocked hush covered the courtyard. Only Mapfarity's wrathful breathing could be heard. Then, disembodied, Lusine's voice floated from the well.

"Jean-Jacques, do not forget that I am the foster-daughter of the King of the Amphibians! If you were to take me with you, I could assure you of safety and a warm welcome in the halls of the Sea-King's Palace!"

"Pah!" said Mapfarity. "That web-footed witch!"

Rastignac did not reply to her. He took the broad silk belt and the sheathed épée from Archambaud and buckled them around his waist. Mapfarity handed him a mucketeer's hat; he clapped that on firmly. Last of all, he took the Skin that the fat egg-stealer had been holding out to him.

For the first time he hesitated. It was his Skin, the one he had been wearing since he was six. It had grown with him, fed off his blood for twenty-two years, clung to him as clothing, censor, and castigator, and parted from him only when he was inside the walls of his own house, went swimming, or, as during the last seven days, when he laid in jail.

A week ago, after they had removed his second Skin, he had felt naked and helpless and cut off from his fellow creatures. But that was a week ago. Since then, as he had remarked to Lusine, he had experienced the birth of a strange feeling. It was, at first, frightening. It made him cling to the bars as if they were the only stable thing in the center of a whirling universe.

Later, when that first giddiness had passed, it was succeeded by another intoxication—the joy of being an individual, the knowledge that he was separate, not a part of a multitude. Without the Skin he could think as he pleased. He did not have a censor.

Now, he was on level ground again, out of the cell. But as soon as he had put that prison-shaft behind him he was faced with the old second Skin.

Archambaud held it out like a cloak in his hands. It looked much like a ragged garment. It was pale and limp and roughly rectangular with four extensions at each corner. When Rastignac put it on his back, it would sink four tiny hollow teeth into his veins and the suckers on the inner surface of its flat body would cling to him. Its long upper extensions would wrap themselves around his shoulders and over his chest; the lower, around his loins and thighs. Soon it would lose its paleness and flaccidity, become pink and slightly convex, pulsing with Rastignac's blood.

V

Rastignac hesitated for a few seconds. Then he allowed the habit of a lifetime to take over. Sighing, he turned his back. In a moment he felt the cold flesh descend over his shoulders and the little bite of the four teeth as they attached the Skin to his shoulders. Then, as his blood poured into the creature he felt it grow warm and strong. It spread out and followed the passages it had long ago been conditioned to follow, wrapped him warmly and lovingly and comfortably. And he knew, though he couldn't feel it, that it was pushing nerves into the grooves along the teeth. Nerves to connect with his.

A minute later he experienced the first of the expected *rapport*. It was nothing that you could put a mental finger on. It was just a diffused tingling and then the sudden consciousness of how the others around him *felt*.

They were ghosts in the background of his mind. Yet, pale and ectoplasmic as they were, they were easily identifiable. Mapfarity loomed above the others, a transparent Colossus radiating streamers of confidence in his clumsy strength. A meat-eater, uncertain about the future, with a hope and trust in Rastignac to show him the right way. And with a strong current of anger against the conqueror who had inflicted the Skin upon him.

Archambaud was a shorter phantom, rolypoly even in his psychic manifestations, emitting bursts of impatience because other people did not talk fast enough to suit him, his mind leaping on ahead of their tongues, his fingers wriggling to wrap themselves around something valuable—preferably the eggs of the golden goose—and a general eagerness to be up and about and onwards. He was one round fidget on two legs, yet a good man for any project requiring action.

Faintly, Rastignac detected the slumbering guard as if he were the tendrils of some plant at the sea-bottom, floating in the green twilight, at peace and unconscious.

And even more faintly he felt Lusine's presence, shielded by the walls of the shaft. Hers was a pale and light hand, one whose fingers tapped a barely heard code of impotent rage and voiceless screaming fear. Yet beneath that anguish was a base of confidence and mockery at others. She might be temporarily upset, but when the chance came for her to do something she would seize it with every ability at her command.

Another radiation dipped into the general picture and out. A wild glowworm had swooped over them and disturbed the smooth reflection built up by the Skins.

This was the way the Skins worked. They penetrated into you and found out what you were feeling and emoting, and then they broadcast it to other closeby Skins, which then projected their hosts' psychosomatic responses. The whole was then integrated so that each Skin-wearer could detect the group-feeling and at the same time, though in a much duller manner, the feeling of the individuals of the *gestalt*.

That wasn't the only function of the Skin. The parasite, created in the bio-factories, had several other social and biological uses.

Rastignac almost fell into a reverie at that point. It was nothing unusual. The effect of the Skins was a slowing-down one. The wearer thought more slowly, acted more leisurely, and was much more contented.

But now, by a deliberate wrenching of himself from the feeling-pattern, Rastignac woke up. There were things to do, and standing around and drinking in the lotus of the group-rapport was not one of them.

He gestured at the prostrate form of the mucketeer. "You didn't hurt him?"

The Ssassaror rumbled, "No. I scratched him with a little venom of the dream-snake. He will sleep for an hour or so. Besides, I would not be allowed to hurt him. You forget that all this is carefully staged by the King's Official Jail-breaker."

"*Me'dt!*" swore Rastignac.

Alarmed, Archambaud said, "What's the matter, Jean-Jacques?"

"Can't we do anything on our own? Must the King meddle in everything?"

"You wouldn't want us to take a chance and have to shed *blood*, would you?" breathed Archambaud.

"What are you carrying those swords for? As a decoration?" Rastignac snarled.

"*Seelahs, m'fweh*," warned Mapfarity. "If you alarm the other guards, you will embarrass them. They will be forced to do their duty and recapture you. And the Jail-breaker would be reprimanded because he had fallen down on his job. He might even get a demotion."

Rastignac was so upset that his Skin, reacting to the negative fields racing over the Skin and the hormone imbalance of his blood, writhed away from his back.

"What are we, a bunch children playing war?"

Mapfarity growled, "We are all God's children, and we mustn't hurt anyone if we can help it."

"Mapfarity, you eat meat!"

"*Voo zavf w'zaw m'fweh*," admitted the Giant. "But it is the flesh of unintelligent creatures. I have not yet shed the blood of any being that can talk with the tongue of Man."

Rastignac snorted and said, "If you stick with me you will some day do that, *m'fweh* Mapfarity. There is no other course. It is inevitable."

"Nature spare me the day! But if it comes it will find Mapfarity unafraid. They do not call me Giant for nothing."

Rastignac sighed and walked ahead. Sometimes he wondered if the members of his underground—or anybody else for that matter—ever realized the grim conclusions formed by the Philosophy of Violence.

The Amphibians, he was sure, did. And they were doing something positive about it. But it was the Amphibians who had driven Rastignac to adopt a Philosophy of Violence.

"*Law*," he said again. "Let's go."

The three of them walked out of the huge courtyard and through the open gate. Nearby stood a short man whose Skin gleamed black-red in the light shed by the two glowworms attached to his shoulders. The Skin was oversized and hung to the ground.

The King's man, however, did not think he was a comic figure.

He sputtered, and the red of his face matched the color of the skin on his back.

"You took long enough," he said accusingly and then, when Rastignac opened his mouth to protest, the Jail-breaker said, "Never mind, never mind. *Sa n'apawt.* The thing is that we get you away fast. The Minister of Ill-Will has doubtless by now received word that an official jail-break is planned for tonight. He will send a company of his mucketeers to intercept you. By coming in advance of the appointed time we shall have time to escape before the official rescue party arrives."

"How much time do we have?" asked Rastignac.

The King's man said, "Let's see. After I escort you through the rooms of the Duke, the King's foster-brother—he is most favorable to the Violent Philosophy, you know, and has petitioned the King to become your official patron, which petition will be considered at the next meeting of the Chamber of Deputies in three months—let's see, where was I? Ah, yes, I escort you through the rooms of the King's brother. You will be disguised as His Majesty's mucketeers, ostensibly looking for the escaped prisoners. From the rooms of the Duke you will be let out through a small door in the wall of the palace itself. A car will be waiting.

"From then on it will be up to you. I suggest, however, that you make a dash for Mapfarity's castle. Follow the *Rue des Nues*; that is your best chance. The mucketeers have been pulled off that boulevard. However, it is possible that Auverpin, the Ill-Will Minister, may see that order and will rescind it, realizing what it means. If he does, I suppose I will see you back in your cell, Rastignac."

He bowed to the Ssassaror and Archambaud and said, "And you two gentlemen will then be with him."

"And then what?" rumbled Mapfarity.

"According to the law, you will be allowed one more jail-break. Any more after that will, of course, be illegal. That is, unthinkable."

Rastignac unsheathed his épée and slashed it at the air. "Let the mucketeers stand in my way," he said fiercely. "I will cut them down with this!"

The Jail-breaker staggered back, hands outthrust.

"Please, Monsieur Rastignac! Please! Don't even talk about it! You know that your philosophy is, as yet, illegal. The shedding of blood is an act that will be regarded with horror throughout the sentient planet. People would think you are an Amphibian!"

"The Amphibians know what they're doing far better than we do," answered Rastignac. "Why do you think they're winning against us Humans?"

Suddenly, before anybody could answer, the sound of blaring horns came from somewhere on the ramparts. Shouts went up; drums began to beat, calling the mucketeers to alert.

And above it all came the roar of a giant Ssassaror voice: "*An Earthship has landed in the sea! And the pilot of the ship is in the hands of the Amphibians!*"

As the meaning of the words seeped into Rastignac's consciousness he made a sudden violent movement—and began to tear the Skin from his body!

VI

Rastignac ran down the steps, out into the courtyard. He seized the Jail-breaker's arm and demanded the key to the grilles. Dazed, the white-faced official meekly and silently handed it to him. Without his Skin Rastignac was no longer fearfully inhibited. If you were forceful enough and did not behave according to the normal pattern you could get just about anything you wanted. The average Man or Ssassaror did not know how to react to his violence. By the time they had recovered from their confusion he could be miles away.

Such a thought flashed through his head as he ran towards the prison wells. At the same time he heard the horn-blasts of the king's mucketeers and knew that he shortly would have a different type of Man to deal with. The mucketeers, closest approach to soldiers in this pacifistic land, wore Skins that conditioned them to be more belligerent than the common citizen. They carried épées and, while it was true that their points were dull and their wielders had never engaged in serious swordsmanship, the mucketeers could be dangerous from a viewpoint of numbers alone.

Mapfarity bellowed, "Jean-Jacques, what are you doing?"

He called back over his shoulder, "I'm taking Lusine with us! She can help us get the Earthman from the Amphibians!"

The Giant lumbered up behind him, threw a rope down to the eager hands of Lusine and pulled her up without effort to the top of the well. A second later, Rastignac leaped upon Mapfarity's back, dug his hands under the upper fringe of the huge Skin and, ignoring its electrical blasts, ripped downwards.

Mapfarity cried out with shock and surprise as his skin flopped on the stones like a devilfish on dry land.

Archambaud ran up then and, without bothering to explain, the Ssassaror and the Man seized him and peeled off *his* artificial hide.

"Now we're all free men!" panted Rastignac. "And the mucketeers have no way of locating us if we hide, nor can they punish us with shocks."

He put the Giant on his right side, Lusine on his left, and the egg-stealer behind him. He removed the Jail-breaker's rapier from his sheath. The official was too astonished to protest.

"*Law, m'zawfa!*" cried Rastignac, parodying in his grotesque French the old Gallic war cry of "*Allons, mes enfants!*"

The King's official came to life and screamed orders at the group of mucketeers who had poured into the courtyard. They halted in confusion. They could not hear him above the roar of horns and thunder of drums and the people sticking their heads out of windows and shouting.

Rastignac scooped up with his épée one of the abandoned Skins flopping on the floor and threw it at the foremost guard. It descended upon the man's head, knocking off his hat and wrapping itself around the head and shoulders. The guard dropped his sword and staggered backwards into the group. At the same time the escapees charged and bowled over their feeble opposition.

It was here that Rastignac drew first blood. The tip of his épée drove past a bewildered mucketeer's blade and entered the fellow's throat just below the chin. It did not penetrate very far because of the dullness of the point. Nevertheless, when Rastignac withdrew his sword he saw blood spurt.

It was the first flower of violence, this scarlet blossom set against the whiteness of a Man's skin.

It would, if he had worn his Skin, have sickened him. Now, he exulted with a shout of triumph.

Lusine swooped up from behind him, bent over the fallen man. Her fingers dipped into the blood and went to her mouth. Greedily, she sucked her fingers.

Rastignac struck her cheek hard with the flat of his hand. She staggered back, her eyes narrow, but she laughed.

The next moments were busy as they entered the castle, knocked down two mucketeers who tried to prevent their passage to the Duke's rooms, then filed across the long suite.

The Duke rose from his writing-desk to greet them. Rastignac, determined to sever all ties and impress the government with the fact that he meant a real violence, snarled at his benefactor, "*Va t'feh fout!*"

The Duke was disconcerted at this harsh command, so obviously impossible to carry out. He blinked and said nothing. The escapees hurried past him to the door that gave exit to the outside. They pushed it open and stepped out into the car that waited for them. A chauffeur leaned against its thin wooden body.

Mapfarity pushed him aside and climbed in. The others followed. Rastignac was the last to get in. He examined in a glance the vehicle they were supposed to make their flight in.

It was as good a car as you could find in the realm. A Renault of the large class, it had a long boat-shaped scarlet body. There wasn't a scratch on it. It had seats for six. And that it had the power to outrun most anything was indicated by the two extra pairs of legs sticking out from the bottom. There were twelve pairs of legs, equine in form and shod with the best steel. It was the kind of vehicle you wanted when you might have to take off across the country. Wheeled cars could go faster on the highway, but this Renault would not be daunted by water, plowed fields, or steep hillsides.

Rastignac climbed into the driver's seat, seized the wheel and pressed his foot down on the accelerator. The nerve-spot beneath the pedal sent a message to the muscles hidden beneath the hood and the legs projecting from the body. The Renault lurched forward, steadied, and began to pick up speed. It entered a broad paved highway. Hooves drummed; sparks shot out from the steel shoes.

Rastignac guided the brainless, blind creature concealed within the body. He was helped by the somatically-generated radar it employed to steer it past obstacles. When he came to the *Rue des Nues*, he slowed it down to a trot. There was no use tiring it out. Halfway up the gentle slope of the boulevard, however, a Ford galloped out from a side-street. Its seats bristled with tall peaked hats with outspread glowworm wings and with drawn épées.

Rastignac shoved the accelerator to the floor. The Renault broke into a gallop. The Ford turned so that it would present its broad side. As there was a fencework of tall shrubbery growing along the boulevard, the Ford was thus able to block most of the passage.

But, just before his vehicle reached the Ford, Rastignac pressed the Jump button. Few cars had this; only sportsmen or the royalty could afford to have such a neural circuit installed. And it did not allow for gradations in leaping. It was an all-or-none reaction; the legs spurned the ground in perfect unison and with every bit of the power in them. There was no holding back.

The nose lifted, the Renault soared into the air. There was a shout, a slight swaying as the trailing hooves struck the heads of mucketeers who had been stupid enough not to duck, and the vehicle landed with a screeching lurch, upright, on the other side of the Ford. Nor did it pause.

Half an hour later Rastignac reined in the car under a large tree whose shadow protected them. "We're well out in the country," he said.

"What do we do now?" asked impatient Archambaud.

"First we must know more about this Earthman," Rastignac answered. "Then we can decide."

VII

Dawn broke through night's guard and spilled a crimson swath on the hills to the East, and the Six Flying Stars faded from sight like a necklace of glowing jewels dipped into an ink bottle.

Rastignac halted the weary Renault on the top of a hill, looked down over the landscape spread out for miles below him. Mapfarity's castle—a tall rose-colored tower of flying buttresses—flashed in the rising sun. It stood on another hill by the sea shore. The country around was a madman's dream of color. Yet to Rastignac every hue sickened the eye. That bright green, for instance, was poisonous; that flaming scarlet was bloody; that pale yellow, rheumy; that velvet black, funeral; that pure white, maggotty.

"Rastignac!" It was Mapfarity's bass, strumming irritation deep in his chest.

"What?"

"What do we do now?"

Jean-Jacques was silent. Archambaud spoke plaintively.

"I'm not used to going without my Skin. There are things I miss. For one thing, I don't know what you're thinking, Jean-Jacques. I don't know whether you're angry at me or love me or are indifferent to me. I don't know where other people *are*. I don't feel the joy of the little animals playing, the freedom of the flight of birds, the ghostly plucking of the growing grass, the sweet stab of the mating lust of the wild-horned apigator, the humming of bees working to build a hive, and the sleepy stupid arrogance of the giant cabbage-eating *deuxnez*. I can feel nothing without the Skin I have worn so long. I feel alone."

Rastignac replied, "You are not alone. I am with you."

Lusine spoke in a low voice, her large brown eyes upon his.

"I, too, feel alone. My Skin is gone, the Skin by which I knew how to act according to the wisdom of my father, the Amphib King. Now that it is gone and I cannot hear his voice through the vibrating tympanum, I do not know what to do."

"At present," replied Rastignac, "you will do as I tell you."

Mapfarity repeated, "What now?"

Rastignac became brisk. He said, "We go to your castle, Giant. We use your smithy to put sharp points on our swords, points to slide through a man's body from front to back. Don't pale! That is what we must do. And then we pick up your goose that lays the golden eggs, for we must have money if we are to act efficiently. After that, we buy—or steal—a boat and we go to wherever the Earthman is held captive. And we rescue him."

"And then?" said Lusine, her eyes shining with emotion.

"What you do then will be up to you. But I am going to leave this planet and voyage with the Earthman to other worlds."

Silence. Then Mapfarity said, "Why leave here?"

"Because there is no hope for this land. Nobody will give up his Skin. *Le Beau Pays* is doomed to a lotus-life. And that is not for me."

Archambaud jerked a thumb at the Amphib girl. "What about her people?"

"They may win, the water-people. What's the difference? It will be just the exchange of one Skin for another. Before I heard of the landing of the Earthman I was going to fight no matter what the cost to me or inevitable defeat. But not now."

Mapfarity's rumble was angry. "Ah, Jean-Jacques, this is not my comrade talking. Are you sure you haven't swallowed your Skin? You talk as if you were inside-out. What is the matter with your brain? Can't you see that it will indeed make a difference if the Amphibs get the upper hand? Can't you see *who* is making the Amphibs behave the way they have been?"

Rastignac urged the Renault towards the rose-colored lacy castle high upon a hill. The vehicle trotted tiredly along the rough and narrow forest path.

"What do you mean?" he said.

"I mean the Amphibs got along fine with the Ssassaror until a new element entered their lives—the Earthmen. Then the antagonising began. What is this new element? It's the Changelings—the mixture of Earthmen and Amphibs or Ssassaror and Terran. Add it up. Turn it around. Look at it from any angle. It is the Changelings who are behind this restlessness—the Human element.

"Another thing. The Amphibs have always had Skins different

from ours. Our factories create our Skins to set up an affinity and communication between their wearers and all of Nature. They are designed to make it easier for every Man to love his neighbor.

"Now, the strange thing about the Amphibs' Skin is that they, too, were once designed to do such things. But in the past thirty or forty years new Skins have been created for one primary purpose—to establish a communication between the Sea-King and his subjects. Not only that, the Skins can be operated at long distances so that the King may punish any disobedient subject. And they are set so that they establish affinity only among the Water-folk, not between them and all of Nature."

"I had gathered some of that during my conversations with Lusine," said Rastignac. "But I did not know it had gone to such lengths."

"Yes, and you may safely bet that the Changelings are behind it."

"Then it is the human element that is corrupting?"

"What else?"

Rastignac said, "Lusine, what do you say to this?"

"I think it is best that you leave this world. Or else turn Changeling-Amphib."

"Why should I join you Amphibians?"

"A man like you could become a Sea-King."

"And drink blood?"

"I would rather drink blood than mate with a Man. Almost, that is. But I would make an exception with you, Jean-Jacques."

If it had been a Land-woman who made such a blunt proposal he would have listened with equanimity. There was no modesty, false or otherwise in the country of the Skin-wearers. But to hear such a thing from a woman whose mouth had drunk the blood of a living man filled him with disgust.

Yet, he had to admit Lusine was beautiful. If she had not been a blood-drinker . . .

Though he lacked his receptive Skin, Mapfarity seemed to sense Rastignac's emotions. He said, "You must not blame her too much, Jean-Jacques. Sea-changelings are conditioned from babyhood to love blood. And for a very definite purpose, too, unnatural though it is. When the time comes for hordes of Changelings to sweep out of the sea and overwhelm the Landfolk, they will have no compunctions about cutting the throats of their fellow-creatures."

Lusine laughed. The rest of them shifted uneasily but did not comment. Rastignac changed the subject.

"How did you find out about the Earthman, Mapfarity?" he said.

The Ssassaror smiled. Two long yellow canines shone wetly; the nose, which had nostrils set in the sides, gaped open; blue sparks shot out from it; at the same time the feathered tufts on the ends of the elephantine ears stiffened and crackled with red-and-blue sparks.

"I have been doing something besides breeding geese to lay golden eggs," he said. "I have set traps for Waterfolk, and I have caught two. These I caged in a dungeon in my castle, and I experimented with them. I removed their Skins and put them on me, and I found out many interesting facts."

He leered at Lusine, who was no longer laughing, and he said, "For instance, I discovered that the Sea-King can locate, talk to, and punish any of his subjects anywhere in the sea or along the coast. He has booster Skins planted all over his realm so that any message he sends will reach the receiver, no matter how far away he is. Moreover, he has conditioned each and every Skin so that, by uttering a certain code-word to which only one particular Skin will respond, he may stimulate it to shock or even to kill its carrier."

Mapfarity continued, "I analyzed those two Skins in my lab and then, using them as models, made a number of duplicates in my fleshforge. They lacked only the nerves that would enable the Sea-King to shock us."

Rastignac smiled his appreciation of this coup. Mapfarity's ears crackled blue sparks of joy, his equivalent of blushing.

"Ah, then you have doubtless listened in to many broadcasts. And you know where the Earthman is located?"

"Yes," said the Giant. "He is in the palace of the Amphib King, upon the island of Kataproimnoin. That is only thirty miles out to the sea."

Rastignac did not know what he would do, but he had two advantages in the Amphibs' Skins and in Lusine. And he burned to get off this doomed planet, this land of men too sunk in false happiness, sloth, and stupidity to see that soon death would come from the water.

He had two possible avenues of escape. One was to use the newly arrived Earthman's knowledge so that the fuels necessary to propel the ferry-rockets could be manufactured. The rockets themselves still stood in a museum. Rastignac had not planned to use them because neither he nor any one else on this planet knew how to make fuel for them. Such secrets had long ago been forgotten.

But now that science was available through the newcomer from Earth, the rockets could be equipped and taken up to one of the Six Flying Stars. The Earthman could study the rocket, determine what was needed in the way of supplies, then it could be outfitted for the long voyage.

An alternative was the Terran's vessel. Perhaps he might invite him to come along in it. . . .

The huge gateway to Mapfarity's castle interrupted his thoughts.

VIII

He halted the Renault, told Archambaud to find the Giant's servant and have him feed their vehicle, rub its legs down with liniment, and examine the hooves for defective shoes.

Archambaud was glad to look up Mapfabvisheen, the Giant's servant, because he had not seen him for a long time. The little Ssassaror had been an active member of the Egg-stealer's Guild until the night three years ago when he had tried to creep into Mapfarity's strongroom. The crafty guildsman had avoided the Giant's traps and there found the two geese squatting upon their bed of minerals.

These fabulous geese made no sound when he picked them up with lead-lined gloves and put them in his bag, also lined with lead-leaf. They were not even aware of him. Laboratory-bred, retort-shaped, their protoplasm a blend of silicon-carbon, unconscious even that they lived, they munched upon lead and other elements, ruminated, gestated, transmuted, and every month, regular as the clockwork march of stars or whirl of electrons, each laid an octagonal egg of pure gold.

Mapfabvisheen had trodden softly from the strongroom and thought himself safe. And then, amazingly, frighteningly, and totally unethically, from his viewpoint, the geese had begun honking loudly!

He had run, but not fast enough. The Giant had come stumbling from his bed in response to the wild clamor and had caught him. And, according to the contract drawn up between the Guild of Egg-stealers and the League of Giants, a guildsman seized within the precincts of a castle must serve the goose's owner for two years. Mapfabvisheen had been greedy; he had tried to take both geese. Therefore, he must wait upon the Giant for a double term.

Afterwards, he found out how he'd been trapped. The egglayers themselves hadn't been honking. Mouthless, they were utterly incapable of that. Mapfarity had fastened a so-called "goose-tracker" to the strong-room's doorway. This device clicked loudly whenever a goose was nearby. It could smell out one even through a lead-leaf-lined bag. When Mapfabvisheen passed underneath it, its clicks woke up a small Skin beside it. The Skin, mostly lung-sac and voice organs, honked its warning. And the dwarf, Mapfabvisheen, began his servitude to the Giant, Mapfarity.

Rastignac knew the story. He also knew that Mapfarity had infected the fellow with the philosophy of Violence and that he was now a good member of his Underground. He was eager to tell him his servitor days were over, that he could now take his place in their band as an equal. Subject, of course, to Rastignac's order.

Mapfabvisheen was stretched out upon the floor and snoring a sour breath. A grey-haired man was slumped on a nearby table. His head, turned to one side, exhibited the same slack-jawed look that the Ssassaror's had, and he flung the ill-smelling gauntlet of his breath at the visitors. He held an empty bottle in one loose hand. Two other bottles lay on the stone floor, one shattered.

Besides the bottles lay the men's Skins. Rastignac wondered why they had not crawled to the halltree and hung themselves up.

"What ails them? What is that smell?" said Mapfarity.

"I don't know," replied Archambaud, "but I know the visitor. He is Father Jules, priest of the Guild of Egg-stealers."

Rastignac raised his queer, bracket-shaped eyebrows, picked up a bottle in which there remained a slight residue, and drank.

"Mon Dieu, it is the sacrament wine!" he cried.

Mapfarity said, "Why would they be drinking that?"

"I don't know. Wake Mapfabvisheen up, but let the good father sleep. He seems tired after his spiritual labors and doubtless deserves a rest."

Doused with a bucket of cold water the little Ssassaror staggered to his feet. Seeing Archambaud, he embraced him. "Ah, Archambaud, old baby-abductor, my sweet goose-bagger, my ears tingle to see you again!"

They did. Red and blue sparks flew off his ear-feathers.

"What is the meaning of this?" sternly interrupted Mapfarity. He pointed at the dirt swept into the corners.

Mapfabvisheen drew himself up to his full dignity, which wasn't much. "Good Father Jules was making his circuits," he said. "You know he travels around the country and hears confession and sings Mass for us poor egg-stealers who have been unlucky enough to fall into the clutches of some rich and greedy and anti-social Giant who is too stingy to hire servants, but captures them instead, and who won't allow us to leave the premises until our servitude is over. . . ."

"Cut it!" thundered Mapfarity. "I can't stand around all day, listening to the likes of you. My feet hurt too much. Anyway, you know I've allowed you to go into town every week-end. Why don't you see a priest then?"

Mapfabvisheen said, "You know very well the closest town is ten kilometers away and it's full of Pantheists. There's not a priest to be found there."

Rastignac groaned inwardly. Always it was thus. You could never hurry these people or get them to regard anything seriously.

Take the case they were wasting their breath on now. Everybody knew the Church had been outlawed a long time ago because it opposed the use of the Skins and certain other practices that went along with it. So, no sooner had that been done than the Ssassarors, anxious to establish their check-and-balance system, had made arrangements through the Minister of Ill-Will to give the Church unofficial legal recognizance.

Then, though the aborigines had belonged to that pantheistical organization known as the Sons of Good And Old Mother Nature, they had all joined the Church of the Terrans. They operated under the theory that the best way to make an institution innocuous was for everybody to sign up for it. Never persecute. That makes it thrive.

Much to the Church's chagrin, the theory worked. How can you fight an enemy who insists on joining you and who will also agree to everything you teach him and then still worship at the other service? Supposedly driven underground, the Church counted almost every Landsman among its supporters from the Kings down.

Every now and then a priest would forget to wear his Skin out-of-doors and be arrested, then released later in an official jail-break. Those who refused to cooperate were forcibly kidnapped, taken to another town and there let loose. Nor did it do the priest any good to proclaim boldly who he was. Everybody pretended not to know he was a fugitive from justice. They insisted on calling him by his official pseudonym.

However, few priests were such martyrs. Generations of Skin-wearing had sapped the ecclesiastical vigor.

The thing that puzzled Rastignac about Father Jules was the sacrament wine. Neither he nor anybody else in L'Bawpfey, as far as he knew, had ever tasted the liquid outside of the ceremony. Indeed, except for certain of the priests, nobody even knew how to make wine.

He shook the priest awake, said, "What's the matter, Father?"

Father Jules burst into tears. "Ah, my boy, you have caught me in my sin. I am a drunkard."

Everybody looked blank. "What does that word *drunkard* mean?"

"It means a man who's damned enough to fill his Skin with alcohol, my boy, fill it until he's no longer a man but a beast."

"Alcohol? What is that?"

"The stuff that's in the wine, my boy. You don't know what I'm talking about because the knowledge was long ago forbidden except to us of the cloth. Cloth, he says! Bah! We go around like everybody, naked except for these extradermal monstrosities which reveal rather than conceal, which not only serve us as clothing but as mentors, parents, censors, interpreters, and, yes, even as priests. Where's a bottle that's not empty? I'm thirsty."

Rastignac stuck to the subject "Why was the making of this alcohol forbidden?"

"How should I know?" said Father Jules. "I'm old, but not so ancient that I came with the Six Flying Stars. . . . Where is that bottle?"

Rastignac was not offended by his crossness. Priests were notorious for being the most ill-tempered, obstreperous, and unstable of men. They were not at all like the clerics of Earth, whom everybody knew from legend had been sweet-tempered, meek, humble, and obedient to authority. But on L'Bawpfey these men of the Church had reason to be out of sorts. Everybody attended Mass, paid their tithes, went to confession, and did not fall asleep during sermons. Everybody believed what the priests told them and were as good as it was possible for human beings to be. So, the priests had no real incentive to work, no evil to fight.

Then why the prohibition against alcohol?

"*Sacre Bleu!*" groaned Father Jules. "Drink as much as I did last night and you'll find out. Never again, I say. Ah, there's another bottle, hidden by a providential fate under my traveling robe. Where's that corkscrew?"

Father Jules swallowed half of the bottle, smacked his lips, picked up his Skin from the floor, brushed off the dirt and said, "I must be going, my sons. I've a noon appointment with the bishop, and I've a good twelve kilometers to travel. Perhaps one of you gentlemen has a car?"

Rastignac shook his head and said he was sorry but their car was tired and had, besides, thrown a shoe. Father Jules shrugged philosophically, put on his Skin and reached out again for the bottle.

Rastignac said, "Sorry, Father. I'm keeping this bottle."

"For what?" asked father Jules.

"Never mind. Say I'm keeping you from temptation."

"Bless you, my son, and may you have a big enough hangover to show you the wickedness of your ways."

Smiling, Rastignac watched the Father walk out. He was not disappointed. The priest had no sooner reached the huge door than his Skin fell off and lay motionless upon the stone.

"Ah," breathed Rastignac. "The same thing happened to Mapfabvisheen when he put his on. There must be something about the wine that deadens the Skins, makes them fall off."

After the padre had left, Rastignac handed the bottle to Mapfarity. "We're dedicated to breaking the law most illegally, brother. So I'm asking you to analyze this wine and find out how to make it."

"Why not ask Father Jules?"

"Because priests are pledged never to reveal the secret. That was one of the original agreements whereby the Church was allowed to remain on L'Bawpfey. Or, at least that's what my parish priest told me. He said it was a good thing, as it removed an evil from man's temptation. He never did say why it was so evil. Maybe he didn't know.

"That doesn't matter. What does matter is that the Church has inadvertently given us a weapon whereby we may free Man from his bondage to the Skins and it has also given itself once again a chance to be really persecuted and to flourish on the blood of its martyrs."

"Blood?" said Lusine, licking her lips. "The Churchmen drink blood?"

Rastignac did not explain. He could be wrong. If so, he'd feel less like a fool if they didn't know what he thought.

Meanwhile, there were the first steps to be taken for the unskinning of an entire planet.

IX

Later that day the mucketeers surrounded the castle but they made no effort to storm it. The following day one of them knocked on the huge front door and presented Mapfarity with a summons requiring them to surrender. The Giant laughed, put the document in his mouth and ate it. The server fainted and had to be revived with a bucket of cold water before he could stagger back to report this tradition-shattering reception.

Rastignac set up his underground so it could be expanded in a hurry. He didn't worry about the blockade because, as was well known, Giants' castles had all sorts of subterranean tunnels and secret exits. He contacted a small number of priests who were willing to work for him. These were congenital rebels who became quite enthusiastic when he told them their activities would result in a fierce persecution of the Church.

The majority, however, clung to their Skins and said they would have nothing to do with this extradermal-less devil. They took pride and comfort in that term. The vulgar phrase for the man who refused to wear his Skin was "devil," and, by law and logic, the Church could not be associated with a devil. As everybody knew, the priests have always been on the side of the angels.

Meanwhile, the Devil's band slipped out of the tunnels and made raids. Their targets were Giants' castles and government treasuries; their loot, the geese. So many raids did they make that the president of the League of Giants and the Business Agent for the Guild of Egg-stealers came to plead with them. And remained to denounce. Rastignac was delighted with their complaints, and, after listening for a while, threw them out.

Rastignac had, like all other Skin-wearers, always accepted the monetary system as a thing of reason and steady balance. But, without his Skin he was able to think objectively and saw its weaknesses.

For some cause buried far in history, the Giants had always had control of the means for making the hexagonal golden coins called *oeufs*. But the Kings, wishing to get control of the golden eggs, had set up that élite branch of the Guild which specialized in abducting the half-living 'geese.' Whenever a thief was successful he turned the goose over to his King. The monarch, in turn, sent a note to the robbed Giant informing him that the government intended to keep the goose to make its own currency. But even though the Giant was making counterfeit geese, the King, in his generosity, would ship to the Giant one out of every thirty eggs laid by the kidnappee.

The note was a polite and well-recognized lie. The Giants made the only genuine gold-egg-laying geese on the planet because the Giants' League alone knew the secret. And the King gave back one-thirtieth of his loot so the Giant could accumulate enough money to buy the materials to create another goose. Which would, possibly, be stolen later on.

Rastignac, by his illegal rape of geese, was making money scarce. Peasants were hanging on to their produce and waiting to sell until prices were at their highest. The government, merchants, the league, the guild, all saw themselves impoverished.

Furthermore, the Amphibs, taking note of the situation, were making raids of their own and blaming them on Rastignac.

He did not care. He was intent on trying to find a way to reach Kataproimnoin and rescue the Earthman so he could take off in the spaceship floating in the harbor. But he knew that he would have to take things slowly, to scout out the land and plan accordingly.

Furthermore, Mapfarity had made him promise he would do his best to set up the Landsmen so they would be able to resist the Waterfolk when the day for war came.

Rastignac made his biggest raid when he and his band stole one moonless night into the capital itself to rob the big Goose House, only an egg's throw away from the Palace and the Ministry of Ill-Will. They put the Goose House guards to sleep with little arrows smeared with dream-snake venom, filled their lead-leaf-lined bags with gold eggs, and sneaked out the back door.

As they left, Rastignac saw a cloaked figure slinking from the back door of the Ministry. Seized with intuition, he tackled the figure. It was an Amphib-changeling. Rastignac struck the Amphib with a venomous arrow before the Water-human could cry out or stab back.

Mapfarity grabbed up the limp Amphib and they raced for the safety of the castle.

They questioned the Amphib, Pierre Pusipremnoos, in the castle. At first silent, he later began talking freely when Mapfarity got a heavy Skin from his fleshforge and put it on the fellow. It was a Skin modeled after those worn by the Water-people, but it differed in that the Giant could control, through another Skin, the powerful neural shocks.

After a few shocks Pierre admitted he was the foster-son of the Amphibian King and that, incidentally, Lusine was his foster-sister. He further stated he was a messenger between the Amphib King and the Ssarraror's Ill-Will Minister.

More shocks extracted the fact that the Minister of Ill-Will, Auverpin, was an Amphib-changeling who was passing himself off as a born Landsman. Not only that, the Human hostages among the Amphibs were about to stage a carefully planned revolt against the born Amphibs. It would kill off about half of them. The rest would then be brought under control of the Master Skin.

When the two stepped from the lab they were attacked by Lusine, knife in hand. She gashed Rastignac in the arm before he knocked her out with an upper-cut. Later, while Mapfarity applied a little jelly-like creature called a *scar-jester* to the wound, Rastignac complained:

"I don't know if I can endure much more of this. I thought the way of Violence would not be hard to follow because I hated the Skins and the Amphibs so much. But it is easier to attack a faceless, hypothetical enemy, or torture him, than the individual enemy. Much easier."

"My brother," boomed the Giant, "if you continue to dwell upon the philosophical implications of your actions you will end up as helpless and confused as the leg-counting centipede. Better not think. Warriors are not supposed to. They lose their keen fighting edge when they think. And you need all of that now."

"I would suppose that thought would sharpen them."

"When issues are simple, yes. But you must remember that the system on this planet is anything but uncomplicated. It was set up to confuse, to keep one always off balance. Just try to keep one thing in mind—the Skins are far more of an impediment to Man than they are a help. Also, that if the Skins don't come off the Amphibs will soon be cutting our throats. The only way to save ourselves is to kill them first. Right?"

"I suppose so," said Rastignac. He stooped and put his hands under the unconscious Lusine's armpits. "Help me put her in a room. We'll keep her locked up until she cools off. Then we'll use her to guide us when we get to Kataproimnoin. Which reminds me—how many gallons of the wine have you made so far?"

X

A week later Rastignac summoned Lusine. She came in frowning, and with her lower lip protruding in a pretty pout.

He said, "Day after tomorrow is the day on which the new Kings are crowned, isn't it?"

Tonelessly she said, "Supposedly. Actually, the present Kings will be crowned again."

Rastignac smiled. "I know. Peculiar, isn't it, how the 'people' always vote the same Kings back into power? However, that isn't what I'm getting at. If I remember correctly, the Amphibs give their King exotic and amusing gifts on coronation day. What do you think would happen if I took a big shipload of bottles of wine and passed it out among the population just before the Amphibs begin their surprise massacre?"

Lusine had seen Mapfarity and Rastignac experimenting with the wine and she had been frightened by the results. Nevertheless, she made a brave attempt to hide her fear now. She spit at him and said, "You mud-footed fool! There are priests who will know what it is! They will be in the coronation crowd."

"Ah, not so! In the first place, you Amphibs are almost entirely Aggressive Pantheists. You have only a few priests, and you will now pay for that omission of wine-tasters. Second, Mapfarity's concoction tastes not at all vinous and is twice as strong."

She spat at him again and spun on her heel and walked out.

That night Rastignac's band and Lusine went through a tunnel which brought them up through a hollow tree about two miles west of the castle. There they hopped into the Renault, which had been kept in a camouflaged garage, and drove to the little port of Marrec. Archambaud had paved their way here with golden eggs and a sloop was waiting for them.

Rastignac took the boat's wheel. Lusine stood beside him, ready to answer the challenge of any Amphib patrol that tried to stop them. As the Amphib-King's foster-daughter, she could get the boat through to the Amphib island without any trouble at all.

Archambaud stood behind her, a knife under his cloak, to make sure she did not try to betray them. Lusine had sworn she could be trusted. Rastignac had answered that he was sure she could be, too, as long as the knife point pricked her back to remind her.

Nobody stopped them. An hour before dawn they anchored in the harbor of Kataproimnoin. Lusine was tied hand and foot inside the cabin. Before Rastignac could scratch her with dream-snake venom, she pleaded, "You could not do this to me, Jean-Jacques, if you loved me."

"Who said anything about loving you?"

"Well, I like that! You said so, you cheat!"

"Oh, *then*! Well, Lusine, you've had enough experience to know that such protestations of tenderness and affection are only inevitable accompaniments of the moment's passion."

For the first time since he had known her he saw Lusine's lower lip tremble and tears come in her eyes. "Do you mean you were only using me?" she sobbed.

"You forget I had good reason to think you were just using *me*. Remember, you're an Amphib, Lusine. Your people can't be trusted. You blood-drinkers are as savage as the little sea-monsters you leave in Human cradles."

"Jean-Jacques, take me with you! I'll do anything you say! I'll even cut my foster-father's throat for you!"

He laughed. Unheeding, she swept on. "I want to be with you, Jean-Jacques! Look, with me to guide you in, my homeland—with my prestige as the Amphib-King's daughter—you can become King yourself after the rebellion. I'd get rid of the Amphib-King for you so there'll be nobody in your way!"

She felt no more guilt than a tigress. She was naive and terrible, innocent and disgusting.

"No, thanks, Lusine." He scratched her with the dream-snake needle. As her eyes closed he said, "You don't understand. All I want to do is voyage to the stars. Being King means nothing to me. The only person I'd trade places with would be the Earthman the Amphibs hold prisoner."

He left her sleeping in the locked cabin.

Noon found them loafing on the great square in front of the Palace of the Two Kings of the Sea and the Islands. All were disguised as Waterfolk. Before they'd left the castle, they had grafted webs between their fingers and toes—just as Amphib-changelings who weren't born with them, did—and they wore the special Amphib Skins that Mapfarity had grown in his fleshforge. These were able to tune in on the Amphibs' wavelengths, but they lacked their shock mechanism.

Rastignac had to locate the Earthman, rescue him, and get him to the spaceship that lay anchored between two wharfs, its sharp nose pointing outwards. A wooden bridge had been built from one of the wharfs to a place halfway up its towering side.

Rastignac could not make out any breaks in the smooth metal that would indicate a port, but reason told him there must be some sort of entrance to the ship at that point.

A guard of twenty Amphibs repulsed any attempt on the crowd's part to get on the bridge.

Rastignac had contacted the harbor-master and made arrangements for workmen to unload his cargo of wine. His freehandedness with the gold eggs got him immediate service even on this general holiday. Once in the square, he and his men uncrated the wine but left the two heavy chests on the wagon which was hitched to a powerful little six-legged Jeep.

They stacked the bottles of wine in a huge pile while the curious crowd in the square encircled them to watch. Rastignac then stood on a chest to survey the scene, so that he could best judge the time to start. There were perhaps seven or eight thousand of all three races there—the Ssassarors, the Amphibs, the Humans—with an unequal portioning of each.

Rastignac, looking for just such a thing, noticed that every non-human Amphib had at least two Humans tagging at his heels.

It would take two Humans to handle an Amphib or a Ssassaror. The Amphibs stood upon their seal-like hind flippers at least six and a half feet tall and weighed about three hundred pounds. The Giant Ssassarors, being fisheaters, had reached the same enormous height as Mapfarity. The Giants were in the minority, as the Amphibs had always preferred stealing Human babies from the Terrans. These were marked for death as much as the Amphibs.

Rastignac watched for signs of uneasiness or hostility between the three groups. Soon he saw the signs. They were not plentiful, but they were enough to indicate an uneasy undercurrent. Three times the guards had to intervene to break up quarrels. The Humans eyed the non-human quarrelers, but made no move to help their Amphib fellows against the Giants. Not only that, they took them aside afterwards and seemed to be reprimanding them. Evidently the order was that everyone was to be on his behavior until the time to revolt. Rastignac glanced at the great tower-clock. "It's an hour before the ceremonies begin," he said to his men. "Let's go."

XI

Mapfarity, who had been loitering in the crowd some distance away, caught Archambaud's signal and slowly, as befit a Giant whose feet hurt, limped towards them. He stopped, scrutinized the pile of bottles, then, in his lion's-roar-at-the-bottom-of-a-well voice said, "Say, what's in these bottles?"

Rastignac shouted back, "A drink which the new Kings will enjoy very much."

"What's that?" replied Mapfarity. "Sea-water?"

The crowd laughed.

"No, it's not water," Rastignac said, "as anybody but a lumbering Giant should know. It is a delicious drink that brings a rare ecstacy upon the drinker. I got the formula for it from an old witch who lives on the shores of far off Apfelabvidanahyew. He told me it had been in his family since the coming of Man to L'Bawpfey. He parted with the formula on condition I make it only for the Kings."

"Will only Their Majesties get to taste this exquisite drink?" bellowed Mapfarity.

"That depends upon whether it pleases Their Majesties to give some to their subjects to celebrate the result of the elections."

Archambaud, also planted in the crowd, shrilled, "I suppose if they do, the big-paunched Amphibs and Giants will get twice as much as us Humans. They always do, it seems."

There was a mutter from the crowd; approbation from the Amphibs, protest from the others.

"That will make no difference," said Rastignac, smiling. "The fascinating thing about this is that an Amphib can drink no more than a Human. That may be why the old man who revealed his secret to me called the drink Old Equalizer."

"Ah, you're skinless," scoffed Mapfarity, throwing the most deadly insult known. "I can out-drink, out-eat, and out-swim any Human here. Here, Amphib, give me a bottle, and we'll see if I'm bragging."

An Amphib captain pushed himself through the throng, waddling clumsily on his flippers like an upright seal.

"No, you don't!" he barked. "Those bottles are intended for the Kings. No commoner touches them, least of all a Human and a Giant."

Rastignac mentally hugged himself. He couldn't have planned a better intervention himself! "Why can't I?" he replied. "Until I make an official presentation, these bottles are mine, not the Kings'. I'll do what I want with them."

"Yeah," said the Amphibs. "That's telling him!"

The Amphib's big brown eyes narrowed and his animal-like face wrinkled, but he couldn't think of a retort. Rastignac at once handed a bottle apiece to each of his comrades. They uncorked and drank and then assumed an ecstatic expression which was a tribute to their acting, for these three bottles held only fruit juice.

"Look here, captain," said Rastignac, "why don't you try a swig yourself? Go ahead. There's plenty. And I'm sure Their Majesties would be pleased to contribute some of it on this joyous occasion. Besides, I can always make more for the Kings.

"As a matter of fact," he added, winking, "I expect to get a pension from the courts as the Kings' Old Equalizer-maker."

The crowd laughed. The Amphib, afraid of losing face, took the bottle—which contained wine rather than fruit juice. After a few long swallows the Amphib's eyes became red and a silly grin curved his thin, black-edged lips. Finally, in a thickening voice, he asked for another bottle.

Rastignac, in a sudden burst of generosity, not only gave him one, but began passing out bottles to the many eager reaching hands. Mapfarity and the two egg-thieves helped him. In a short time, the pile of bottles had dwindled to a fourth of its former height. When a mixed group of guards strode up and demanded to know what the commotion was about, Rastignac gave them some of the bottles.

Meanwhile, Archambaud slipped off into the mob. He lurched into an Amphib, said something nasty about his ancestors, and pulled his knife. When the Amphib lunged for the little man, Archambaud jumped back and shoved a Human-Amphib into the giant flipper-like arms.

Within a minute the square had erupted into a fighting mob. Staggering, red-eyed, slur-tongued, their long-repressed hostility against each other, released by the liquor which their bodies were unaccustomed to, Human, Ssassaror and Amphib fell to with the utmost will, slashing, slugging, fighting with everything they had.

None of them noticed that every one who had drunk from the bottles had lost his Skin. The Skins had fallen off one by one and lay motionless on the pavement where they were kicked or stepped upon. Not one Skin tried to crawl back to its owner because they were all nerve-numbed by the wine.

Rastignac, seated behind the wheel of the Jeep, began driving as best he could through the battling mob. After frequent stops he halted before the broad marble steps that ran like a stairway to heaven, up and up before it ended on the Porpoise Porch of the Palace. He and his gang were about to take the two heavy chests off the wagon when they were transfixed by a scene before them.

A score of dead Humans and Amphibs lay on the steps, evidence of the fierce struggle that had taken place between the guards of the two monarchs. Evidently the King had heard of the riot and hastened outside. There the Amphib-changeling King had apparently realized that the rebellion was way ahead of schedule, but he had attacked the Amphib King anyway.

And he had won, for his guardsmen held the struggling flipper-footed Amphib ruler down while two others bent his head back over a step. The Changeling-King himself, still clad in the coronation robes, was about to draw his long ceremonial knife across the exposed and palpitating throat of the Amphib King.

This in itself was enough to freeze the onlookers. But the sight of Lusine running up the stairway towards the rulers added to their paralysis. She had a knife in her hand and was holding it high as she ran toward her foster-father, the Amphib King.

Mapfarity groaned, but Rastignac said, "It doesn't matter that she has escaped. We'll go ahead with our original plan."

They began unloading the chests while Rastignac kept an eye on Lusine. He saw her run up, stop, say a few words to the Amphib King, then kneel and stab him, burying the knife in his jugular vein. Then, before anybody could stop her she had applied her mouth to the cut in his neck.

The Human-King kicked her in the ribs and sent her rolling down the steps. Rastignac saw correctly that it was not her murderous deed that caused his reaction. It was because she had dared to commit it without his permission and had also drunk the royal blood first.

He further noted with grim satisfaction that when Lusine recovered from the blow and ran back up to talk to the King, he ignored her. She pointed at the group around the wagon but he dismissed her with a wave of his hand. He was too busy gloating over his vanquished rival lying at his feet.

The plotters hoisted the two chests and staggered up the steps. The King passed them as he went down with no more than a curious glance. Gifts had been coming up those steps all day for the King, so he undoubtedly thought of them only as more gifts. So Rastignac and his men walked past the knives of the guards as if they had nothing to fear.

Lusine stood alone at the top of the steps. She was in a half-crouch, knife ready. "I'll kill the King and I'll drink from his throat!" she cried hoarsely. "No man kicks me except for love. Has he forgotten that I am the foster-daughter of the Amphib King?"

Rastignac felt revulsion but he had learned by now that those who deal in violence and rebellion must march with strange steppers.

"Bear a hand here," he said, ignoring her threat.

Meekly she grabbed hold of a chest's corner. To his further questioning, she replied that the Earthman who had landed in the ship was held in a suite of rooms in the west wing. Their trip thereafter was fast and direct. Unopposed, they carted the chests to the huge room where the Master Skin was kept.

There they found ten frantic bio-technicians excitedly trying to determine why the great extraderm—the Master Skin through which all individual Skins were controlled—was not broadcasting properly. They had no way as yet of knowing that it was operating perfectly but that the little Skins upon the Amphibs and their hostage Humans were not shocking them into submission because they were lying in a wine-stupor on the ground. No one had told them that the Skins, which fed off the bloodstream of their hosts, had become anesthetized from the alcohol and failed any longer to react to their Master Skin.

That, of course, applied only to those Skins in the square that were drunk from the wine. Elsewhere all over the kingdom, Amphibs writhed in agony and Ssassarors and Terrans were taking advantage of their helplessness to cut their throats. But not here, where the crux of the matter was.

XII

The Landsmen rushed the techs and pushed them into the great chemical vat in which the twenty-five hundred foot square Master Skin floated. Then they uncrated the lead-leaf-lined bags filled with stolen geese and emptied them into the nutrient fluid. According to Mapfarity's calculations, the radio-activity from the silicon-carbon geese should kill the big Skin within a few days. When a new one was grown, that, too, would die. Unless the Amphib guessed what was wrong and located the geese on the bottom of the ten-foot deep tank, they would not be able to stop the process. That did not seem likely.

In either case, it was necessary that the Master Skin be put out of temporary commission, at least, so the Amphibs over the Kingdom could have a fighting chance. Mapfarity plunged a hollow harpoon into the isle of floating protoplasm and through a tube connected to that poured into the Skin three gallons of the dream-snake venom. That was enough to knock it out for an hour or two. Meanwhile, if the Amphibs had any sense at all, they'd have rid themselves of their extraderms.

They left the lab and entered the west wing. As they trotted up the long winding corridors Lusine said, "Jean-Jacques, what do you plan on doing now? Will you try to make yourself King of the Terrans and fight us Amphibs?" When he said nothing she went on. "Why don't you kill the Amphib-changeling King and take over here? I could help you do that. You could then have all of L'Bawpfey in your power."

He shot her a look of contempt and cried, "Lusine, can't you get it through that thick little head of yours that everything I've done has been done so that I can win one goal: reach the Flying Stars? If I can get the Earthman to his ship I'll leave with him and not set foot again for years on this planet. Maybe never again."

She looked stricken. "But what about the war here?" she asked.

"There are a few men among the Landfolk who are capable of leading in wartime. It will take strong men, and there are very few like me, I admit, but—oh, oh, opposition!" He broke off at sight of the six guards who stood before the Earthman's suite.

Lusine helped, and within a minute they had slain three and chased away the others. Then they burst through the door—and Rastignac received another shock.

The occupant of the apartment was a tiny and exquisitely formed redhead with large blue eyes and very unmasculine curves!

"I thought you said Earth*man*?" protested Rastignac to the Giant who came lumbering along behind them.

"Oh, I used that in the generic sense," Mapfarity replied. "You didn't expect me to pay any attention to sex, did you? I'm not interested in the gender of you Humans, you know."

There was no time for reproach. Rastignac tried to explain to the Earthwoman who he was, but she did not understand him. However, she did seem to catch on to what he wanted and seemed reassured by his gestures. She picked up a large book from a table and, hugging it to her small, high and rounded bosom, went with him out the door.

They raced from the palace and descended onto the square. Here they found the surviving Amphibs clustered into a solid phalanx and fighting, bloody step by step, towards the street that led to the harbor.

Rastignac's little group skirted the battle and started down the steep avenue toward the harbor. Halfway down he glanced back and saw that nobody as yet was paying any attention to them. Nor was there anybody on the street to bother them, though the pavement was strewn with Skins and bodies. Apparently, those who'd lived through the first savage mêlée had gone to the square.

They ran onto the wharf. The Earthwoman motioned to Rastignac that she knew how to open the spaceship, but the Amphibs didn't. Moreover, if they did get in, they wouldn't know how to operate it. She had the directions for so doing in the book hugged so desperately to her chest. Rastignac surmised she hadn't told the Amphibs about that. Apparently they hadn't, as yet, tried to torture the information from her.

Therefore, her telling him about the book indicated she trusted him.

Lusine said, "Now what, Jean-Jacques? Are you still going to abandon this planet?"

"Of course," he snapped.

"Will you take me with you?"

He had spent most of his life under the tutelage of his Skin, which ensured that others would know when he was lying. It did not come easy to hide his true feelings. So a habit of a lifetime won out.

"I will not take you," he said. "In the first place, though you may have some admirable virtues, I've failed to detect one. In the second place, I could not stand your blood-drinking nor your murderous and totally immoral ways."

"But, Jean-Jacques, I will give them up for you!"

"Can the shark stop eating fish?"

"You would leave Lusine, who loves you as no Earthwoman could, and go with that—that pale little doll I could break with my hands?"

"Be quiet," he said. "I have dreamed of this moment all my life. Nothing can stop me now."

They were on the wharf beside the bridge that ran up the smooth side of the starship. The guard was no longer there, though bodies showed that there had been reluctance on the part of some to leave.

They let the Earthwoman precede them up the bridge.

Lusine suddenly ran ahead of him, crying, "If you won't have me, you won't have her, either! Nor the stars!"

Her knife sank twice into the Earthwoman's back. Then, before anybody could reach her, she had leaped off the bridge and into the harbor.

Rastignac knelt beside the Earthwoman. She held out the book to him, then she died. He caught the volume before it struck the wharf.

"My God! My God!" moaned Rastignac, stunned with grief and shock and sorrow. Sorrow for the woman and shock at the loss of the ship and the end of his plans for freedom.

Mapfarity ran up then and took the book from his nerveless hand. "She indicated that this is a manual for running the ship," he said. "All is not lost."

"It will be in a language we don't know," Rastignac whispered.

Archambaud came running up, shrilled, "The Amphibs have broken through and are coming down the street! Let's get to our boat before the whole blood-thirsty mob gets here!"

Mapfarity paid him no attention. He thumbed through the book, then reached down and lifted Rastignac from his crouching position by the corpse.

"There's hope yet, Jean-Jacques," he growled. "This book is printed with the same characters as those I saw in a book owned by a priest I knew. He said it was in Hebrew, and that it was the Holy Book in the original Earth language. This woman must be a citizen of the Republic of Israeli, which I understand was rising to be a great power on Earth at the time you French left.

"Perhaps the language of this woman has changed somewhat from the original tongue, but I don't think the alphabet has. I'll bet that if we get this to a priest who can read it—there are only a few left—he can translate it well enough for us to figure out everything."

They walked to the wharf's end and climbed down a ladder to a platform where a dory was tied up. As they rowed out to their sloop Mapfarity said:

"Look, Rastignac, things aren't as bad as they seem. If you haven't the ship nobody else has, either. And you alone have the key to its entrance and operation. For that you can thank the Church, which has preserved the ancient wisdom for emergencies which it couldn't forsee, such as this. Just as it kept the secret of wine, which will eventually be the greatest means for delivering our people from their bondage to the Skins and, thus enable them to fight the Amphibs back instead of being slaughtered.

"Meanwhile, we've a battle to wage. You will have to lead it. Nobody else but the Skinless Devil has the prestige to make the people gather around him. Once we accuse the Minister of Ill-Will of treason and jail him, without an official Breaker to release him, we'll demand a general election. You'll be made King of the Ssassaror; I, of the Terrans. That is inevitable, for we are the only skinless men and, therefore, irresistible. After the war is won, we'll leave for the stars. How do you like that?"

Rastignac smiled. It was weak, but it was a smile. His bracket-shaped eyebrows bent into their old sign of determination.

"You are right," he replied. "I have given it much thought. A man has no right to leave his native land until he's settled his problems here. Even if Lusine hadn't killed the Earthwoman and I had sailed away, my conscience wouldn't have given me any rest. I would have known I had abandoned the fight in the middle of it. But now that I have stripped myself of my Skin—which was a substitute for a conscience—and now that I am being forced to develop my own inward conscience, I must admit that immediate flight to the stars would have been the wrong thing."

The pleased and happy Mapfarity said, "And you must also admit, Rastignac, that things so far have had a way of working out for the best. Even Lusine, evil as she was, has helped towards the general good by keeping you on this planet. And the Church, though it has released once again the old evil of alcohol, has done more good by so doing than. . . ."

But here Rastignac interrupted to say he did not believe in this particular school of thought, and so, while the howls of savage warriors drifted from the wharfs, while the structure of their world crashed around them, they plunged into that most violent and circular of all whirlpools—the Discussion Philosophical.

www.ingramcontent.com/pod-product-compliance
Lightning Source LLC
Chambersburg PA
CBHW050801250626
47155CB00005B/2166

9 781434 410054

DESPOILERS OF THE GOLDEN EMPIRE!

The commander jerked around swiftly as one of the natives grabbed hold of the carrier and tried to hack at the commander with a bronze sword. The commander spitted him neatly on his blade and withdrew it just in time to parry another attack from the other side.

By this time, the reinforcements from the other parts of the village were beginning to come in from the side streets, but they were a little late. The warriors in the square—what was left of them—had panicked. In an effort to get away from the terrible monsters with their deadly blades and their fire-spitting weapons, they were leaving by the same channels that the reinforcements were coming in by, and the resultant jam-up was disastrous. The panic communicated itself like wildfire, but no one could move fast enough to get away from the sweeping, stabbing, glittering blades of the invading Earthmen.

"All right," the commander yelled, "we've got 'em on the run now! Break up into squads of three and clear those streets! Clear 'em out! Keep 'em moving!"

After that, it was the work of minutes to clear the town.

The commander brought his carrier to a dead stop, reached out with his sword, and snagged a bit of cloth from one of the fallen native warriors. He began to wipe the blade of his weapon as Lieutenant commander Hernan pulled up beside him.

"Casualties?" the commander asked Hernan without looking up from his work.

"Six wounded, no dead," said Hernan. "Or did you want me to count the aliens, too?"

DESPOILERS
OF THE
GOLDEN EMPIRE

RANDALL GARRETT

WILDSIDE PRESS

DESPOILERS OF THE GOLDEN EMPIRE

Originally published in *Astounding Science Fiction,* March 1959, under the pseudonym "David Gordon."

Cover by Eugene Ivanov.

Published by Wildside Press, LLC in 2010.

DESPOILERS
OF THE
GOLDEN EMPIRE

I

In the seven centuries that had elapsed since the Second Empire had been founded on the shattered remnants of the First, the nobles of the Imperium had come slowly to realize that the empire was not to be judged by the examples of its predecessor. The First Empire had conquered most of the known universe by political intrigue and sheer military strength; it had fallen because that same propensity for political intrigue had gained over every other strength of the Empire, and the various branches and sectors of the First Empire had begun to use it against one another.

The Second Empire was politically unlike the First; it tried to balance a centralized government against the autonomic governments of the various sectors, and had almost succeeded in doing so.

But, no matter how governed, there are certain essentials which are needed by any governmental organization.

Without power, neither Civilization nor the Empire could hold itself together, and His Universal Majesty, the Emperor Carl, well knew it. And power was linked solidly to one element, one metal, without which Civilization would collapse as surely as if it had been blasted out of existence. Without the power metal, no ship could move or even be built; without it, industry would come to a standstill.

In ancient times, even as far back as the early Greek and Roman civilizations, the metal had been known, but it had been used, for the most part, as decoration and in the manufacture of jewelry. Later, it had been coined as money.

It had always been relatively rare, but now, weight for weight, atom for atom, it was the most valuable element on Earth. Indeed, the most valuable in the known universe.

The metal was Element Number Seventy-nine—gold.

To the collective mind of the Empire, gold was the prime object in any kind of mining exploration. The idea of drilling for petroleum, even if it had been readily available, or of mining coal or uranium would have been dismissed as impracticable and even

worse than useless.

Throughout the Empire, research laboratories worked tirelessly at the problem of transmuting commoner elements into Gold-197, but thus far none of the processes was commercially feasible. There was still, after thousands of years, only one way to get the power metal: extract it from the ground.

So it was that, across the great gulf between the worlds, ship after ship moved in search of the metal that would hold the far-flung colonies of the Empire together. Every adventurer who could manage to get aboard was glad to be cooped up on a ship during the long months it took to cross the empty expanses, was glad to endure the hardships on alien terrain, on the chance that his efforts might pay off a thousand or ten thousand fold.

Of these men, a mere handful were successful, and of these one or two stand well above the rest. And for sheer determination, drive, and courage, for the will to push on toward his goal, no matter what the odds, a certain Commander Frank had them all beat.

II

Before you can get a picture of the commander—that is, as far as his personality goes—you have to get a picture of the man physically.

He was enough taller than the average man to make him stand out in a crowd, and he had broad shoulders and a narrow waist to match. He wasn't heavy; his was the hard, tough, wirelike strength of a steel cable. The planes of his tanned face showed that he feared neither exposure to the elements nor exposure to violence; it was seamed with fine wrinkles and the thin white lines that betray scar tissue. His mouth was heavy-lipped, but firm, and the lines around it showed that it was unused to smiling. The commander could laugh, and often did—a sort of roaring explosion that burst forth suddenly whenever something struck him as particularly uproarious. But he seldom just smiled; Commander Frank rarely went halfway in anything.

His eyes, like his hair, were a deep brown—almost black, and they were set well back beneath heavy brows that tended to frown most of the time.

Primarily, he was a military man. He had no particular flair for science, and, although he had a firm and deep-seated grasp of the essential philosophy of the Universal Assembly, he had no inclination towards the kind of life necessarily led by those who would become higher officers of the Assembly. It was enough that the Assembly was behind him; it was enough to know that he was a member of the only race in the known universe which had a working knowledge of the essential, basic Truth of the Cosmos. With a weapon like that, even an ordinary soldier had little to fear, and Commander Frank was far from being an ordinary soldier.

He had spent nearly forty of his sixty years of life as an explorer-soldier for the Emperor, and during that time he'd kept his eyes open for opportunity. Every time his ship had landed, he'd watched and listened and collected data. And now he knew.

If his data were correct—and he was certain that they were—he had found his strike. All he needed was the men to take it.

III

The expedition had been poorly outfitted and undermanned from the beginning. The commander had been short of money at the outset, having spent almost all he could raise on his own, plus nearly everything he could beg or borrow, on his first two probing expeditions, neither of which had shown any real profit.

But they *had* shown promise; the alien population of the target which the commander had selected as his personal claim wore gold as ornaments, but didn't seem to think it was much above copper in value, and hadn't even progressed to the point of using it as coinage. From the second probing expedition, he had brought back two of the odd-looking aliens and enough gold to show that there must be more where that came from.

The old, hopeful statement, "There's gold in them thar hills," should have brought the commander more backing than he got, considering the Empire's need of it and the commander's evidence that it was available; but people are always more ready to bet on a sure thing than to indulge in speculation. Ten years before, a strike had been made in a sector quite distant from the commander's own find, and most of the richer nobles of the Empire preferred to back an established source of the metal than to sink money into what might turn out to be the pursuit of a wild goose.

Commander Frank, therefore, could only recruit men who were willing to take a chance, who were willing to risk anything, even their lives, against tremendously long odds.

And, even if they succeeded, the Imperial Government would take twenty per cent of the gross without so much as a by-your-leave. There was no other market for the metal except back home, so the tax could not be avoided; gold was no good whatsoever in the uncharted wilds of an alien world.

Because of his lack of funds, the commander's expedition was not only dangerously undermanned, but illegally so. It was only by means of out-and-out trickery that he managed to evade the official inspection and leave port with too few men and too little equipment.

There wasn't a scientist worthy of the name in the whole outfit, unless you call the navigator, Captain Bartholomew, an astronomer, which is certainly begging the question. There was no anthropologist aboard to study the semibarbaric civilization of the natives; there was no biologist to study the alien flora and fauna. The closest thing the commander had to physicists were engineers who could take care of the ship itself—specialist technicians, nothing more.

There was no need for armament specialists; each and every man was a soldier, and, as far as his own weapons went, an ordnance expert. As far as Commander Frank was concerned, that was enough. It had to be.

Mining equipment? He took nothing but the simplest testing apparatus. How, then, did he intend to get the metal that the Empire was screaming for?

The commander had an answer for that, too, and it was as simple as it was economical. The natives would get it for him.

They used gold for ornaments, therefore, they knew where the gold could be found. And, therefore, they would bloody well dig it out for Commander Frank.

IV

Due to atmospheric disturbances, the ship's landing was several hundred miles from the point the commander had originally picked for the debarkation of his troops. That meant a long, forced march along the coast and then inland, but there was no help for it; the ship simply wasn't built for atmospheric navigation.

That didn't deter the commander any. The orders rang through the ship: "All troops and carriers prepare for landing!"

Half an hour later, they were assembled outside the ship, fully armed and armored, and with full field gear. The sun, a yellow G-O star, hung hotly just above the towering mountains to the east. The alien air smelled odd in the men's nostrils, and the weird foliage seemed to rustle menacingly. In the distance, the shrieks of alien fauna occasionally echoed through the air.

A hundred and eighty-odd men and some thirty carriers stood under the tropic blaze for forty-five minutes while the commander checked over their equipment with minute precision. Nothing faulty or sloppy was going into that jungle with him if he could prevent it.

When his hard eyes had inspected every bit of equipment, when he had either passed or ordered changes in the manner of its carrying or its condition, when he was fully satisfied that every weapon was in order—then, and only then, did he turn his attention to the men themselves.

He climbed atop a little hillock and surveyed them carefully, letting his penetrating gaze pass over each man in turn. He stood there, his fists on his hips, with the sunlight gleaming from his burnished armor, for nearly a full minute before he spoke.

Then his powerful voice rang out over the assembled adventurers.

"My comrades-at-arms! We have before us a world that is ours for the taking! It contains more riches than any man on Earth ever dreamed existed, and those riches, too, are ours for the taking. It isn't going to be a picnic, and we all knew that when we came.

There are dangers on every side—from the natives, from the animals and plants, and from the climate.

"But there is not one of these that cannot be overcome by the onslaught of brave, courageous, and determined men!

"Ahead of us, we will find the Four Horsemen of the Apocalypse arrayed against our coming—Famine, Pestilence, War, and Death. Each and all of these we must meet and conquer as brave men should, for at their end we will find wealth and glory!"

A cheer filled the air, startling the animals in the forest into momentary silence.

The commander stilled it instantly with a raised hand.

"Some of you know this country from our previous expeditions together. Most of you will find it utterly strange. And not one of you knows it as well as I do.

"In order to survive, you must—and *will*—follow my orders to the letter—and beyond.

"First, as to your weapons. We don't have an unlimited supply of charges for them, so there will be no firing of any power weapons unless absolutely necessary. You have your swords and your pikes—use them."

Several of the men unconsciously gripped the hafts of the long steel blades at their sides as he spoke the words, but their eyes never left the commanding figure on the hummock.

"As for food," he continued, "we'll live off the land. You'll find that most of the animals are edible, but stay away from the plants unless I give the O.K.

"We have a long way to go, but, by Heaven, I'm going to get us there alive! Are you with me?"

A hearty cheer rang from the throats of the men. They shouted the commander's name with enthusiasm.

"All right!" he bellowed. "There is one more thing! Anyone who wants to stay with the ship can do so; anyone who feels too ill to make it should consider it his duty to stay behind, because sick men will simply hold us up and weaken us more than if they'd been left behind. Remember, we're not going to turn back as a body, and an individual would never make it alone." He paused.

"Well?"

Not a man moved. The commander grinned—not with humor, but with satisfaction. "All right, then: let's move out."

V

Of them all, only a handful, including the commander, had any real knowledge of what lay ahead of them, and that knowledge only pertained to the periphery of the area the intrepid band of adventurers were entering. They knew that the aliens possessed a rudimentary civilization—they did not, at that time, realize they were entering the outposts of a powerful barbaric empire—an empire almost as well-organized and well-armed as that of First Century Rome, and, if anything, even more savage and ruthless.

It was an empire ruled by a single family who called themselves the Great Nobles; at their head was the Greatest Noble—the Child of the Sun Himself. It has since been conjectured that the Great Nobles were mutants in the true sense of the word; a race apart from their subjects. It is impossible to be absolutely sure at this late date, and the commander's expedition, lacking any qualified geneticists or genetic engineers, had no way of determining—and, indeed, no real *interest* in determining—whether this was or was not true. None the less, historical evidence seems to indicate the validity of the hypothesis.

Never before—not even in ancient Egypt—had the historians ever seen a culture like it. It was an absolute monarchy that would have made any Medieval king except the most saintly look upon it in awe and envy. The Russians and the Germans never even approached it. The Japanese tried to approximate it at one time in their history, but they failed.

Secure in the knowledge that theirs was the only civilizing force on the face of the planet, the race of the Great Nobles spread over the length of a great continent, conquering the lesser races as they went.

Physically, the Great Nobles and their lesser subjects were quite similar. They were, like the commander and his men, human in every sense of the word. That this argues some ancient, prehistoric migration across the empty gulfs that separate the worlds cannot be denied, but when and how that migration took place are data lost in the mists of time. However it may have happened, the

fact remains that these people *were* human. As someone observed in one of the reports written up by one of the officers: "They could pass for Indians, except their skins are of a decidedly redder hue."

The race of the Great Nobles held their conquered subjects in check by the exercise of two powerful forces: religion and physical power of arms. Like the feudal organizations of Medieval Europe, the Nobles had the power of life and death over their subjects, and to a much greater extent than the European nobles had. Each family lived on an allotted parcel of land and did a given job. Travel was restricted to a radius of a few miles. There was no money; there was no necessity for it, since the government of the Great Nobles took all produce and portioned it out again according to need. It was communism on a vast and—incomprehensible as it may seem to the modern mind—*workable* scale. Their minds were as different from ours as their bodies were similar; the concept "freedom" would have been totally incomprehensible to them.

They were sun-worshipers, and the Greatest Noble was the Child of the Sun, a godling subordinate only to the Sun Himself. Directly under him were the lesser Great Nobles, also Children of the Sun, but to a lesser extent. They exercised absolute power over the conquered peoples, but even they had no concept of freedom, since they were as tied to the people as the people were tied to them. It was a benevolent dictatorship of a kind never seen before or since.

At the periphery of the Empire of the Sun-Child lived still unconquered savage tribes, which the Imperial forces were in the process of slowly taking over. During the centuries, tribe after tribe had fallen before the brilliant leadership of the Great Nobles and the territory of the Empire had slowly expanded until, at the time the invading Earthmen came, it covered almost as much territory as had the Roman Empire at its peak.

The Imperial Army, consisting of upwards of fifty thousand troops, was extremely mobile in spite of the handicap of having no form of transportation except their own legs. They had no cavalry; the only beast of burden known to them—the flame-beasts—

were too small to carry more than a hundred pounds, in spite of their endurance. But the wide, smooth roads that ran the length and breadth of the Empire enabled a marching army to make good time, and messages carried by runners in relays could traverse the Empire in a matter of days, not weeks.

And into this tight-knit, well-organized, powerful barbaric world marched Commander Frank with less than two hundred men and thirty carriers.

VI

It didn't take long for the men to begin to chafe under the constant strain of moving through treacherous and unfamiliar territory. And the first signs of chafing made themselves apparent beneath their armor.

Even the best designed armor cannot be built to be worn for an unlimited length of time, and, at first, the men could see no reason for the order. They soon found out.

One evening, after camp had been made, one young officer decided that he had spent his last night sleeping in full armor. It was bad enough to have to march in it, but sleeping in it was too much. He took it off and stretched, enjoying the freedom from the heavy steel. His tent was a long way from the center of camp, where a small fire flickered, and the soft light from the planet's single moon filtered only dimly through the jungle foliage overhead. He didn't think anyone would see him from the commander's tent.

The commander's orders had been direct and to the point: "You will wear your armor at all times; you will march in it, you will eat in it, you will sleep in it. During such times as it is necessary to remove a part of it, the man doing so will make sure that he is surrounded by at least two of his companions in full armor. There will be no exceptions to this rule!"

The lieutenant had decided to make himself an exception.

He turned to step into his tent when a voice came out of the nearby darkness.

"Hadn't you better get your steel plates back on before the commander sees you?"

The young officer turned quickly to see who had spoken. It was another of the junior officers.

"Mind your own business," snapped the lieutenant.

The other grinned sardonically. "And if I don't?"

There had been bad blood between these two for a long time; it was an enmity that went back to a time even before the expedition had begun. The two men stood there for a long moment, the light from the distant fire flickering uncertainly against their bodies.

The young officer who had removed his armor had not been foolish enough to remove his weapons too; no sane man did that in hostile territory. His hand went to the haft of the blade at his side.

"If you say a single word—"

Instinctively, the other dropped his hand to his own sword.

"Stop! Both of you!"

And stop they did; no one could mistake the crackling authority in that voice. The commander, unseen in the moving, dim light, had been circling the periphery of the camp, to make sure that all was well. He strode toward the two younger men, who stood silently, shocked into immobility. The commander's sword was already in his hand.

"I'll spit the first man that draws a blade," he snapped.

His keen eyes took in the situation at a glance.

"Lieutenant, what are you doing out of armor?"

"It was hot, sir, and I—"

"Shut up!" The commander's eyes were dangerous. "An asinine statement like that isn't even worth listening to! Get that armor back on! *Move!*"

He was standing approximately between the two men, who had been four or five yards apart. When the cowed young officer took a step or two back toward his tent, the commander turned toward the other officer. "And as for you, if—"

He was cut off by the yell of the unarmored man, followed by the sound of his blade singing from its sheath.

The commander leaped backwards and spun, his own sword at the ready, his body settling into a swordsman's crouch.

But the young officer was not drawing against his superior. He was hacking at something ropy and writhing that squirmed on the ground as the lieutenant's blade bit into it. Within seconds, the serpentine thing gave a convulsive shudder and died.

The lieutenant stepped back clumsily, his eyes glazing in the flickering light. "Dropped from th' tree," he said thickly. "Bit me."

His hand moved to a dark spot on his chest, but it never reached its goal. The lieutenant collapsed, crumpling to the ground.

The commander walked over, slammed the heel of his heavy boot hard down on the head of the snaky thing, crushing it. Then he returned his blade to its sheath, knelt down by the young man, and turned him over on his face.

The commander's own face was grim.

By this time, some of the nearby men, attracted by the yell, had come running. They came to a stop as they saw the tableau before them.

The commander, kneeling beside the corpse, looked up at them. With one hand, he gestured at the body. "Let this be a lesson to all of you," he said in a tight voice. "This man died because he took off his armor. That"—he pointed at the butchered reptile—"thing is full of as deadly a poison as you'll ever see, and it can move like lightning. *But it can't bite through steel!*

"Look well at this man and tell the others what you saw. I don't want to lose another man in this idiotic fashion."

He stood up and gestured.

"Bury him."

VII

They found, as they penetrated deeper into the savage-infested hinterlands of the Empire of the Great Nobles, that the armor fended off more than just snakes. Hardly a day passed but one or more of the men would hear the sharp *spang!* of a blowgun-driven dart as it slammed ineffectually against his armored back or chest. At first, some of the men wanted to charge into the surrounding forest, whence the darts came, and punish the sniping aliens, but the commander would have none of it.

"Stick together," he ordered. "They'll do worse to us if we're split up in this jungle. Those blowgun darts aren't going to hurt you as long as they're hitting steel. Ignore them and keep moving."

They kept moving.

Around them, the jungle chattered and muttered, and, occasionally, screamed. Clouds of insects, great and small, hummed and buzzed through the air. They subsided only when the drizzling rains came, and then lifted again from their resting places when the sun came out to raise steamy vapors from the moist ground.

It was not an easy march. Before many days had passed, the men's feet were cracked and blistered from the effects of fungus, dampness, and constant marching. The compact military marching order which had characterized the first few days of march had long since deteriorated into a straggling column, where the weaker were supported by the stronger.

Three more men died. One simply dropped in his tracks. He was dead before anyone could touch him. Insect bite? Disease? No one knew.

Another had been even less fortunate. A lionlike carnivore had leaped on him during the night and clawed him badly before one of his companions blasted the thing with a power weapon. Three days later, the wounded man was begging to be killed; one arm and one leg were gangrenous. But he died while begging, thus sparing any would-be executioner from an unpleasant duty.

The third man simply failed to show up for roll call one morn-

ing. He was never seen again.

But the rest of the column, with dauntless courage, followed the lead of their commander.

It was hard to read their expressions, those reddened eyes that peered at him from swollen, bearded faces. But he knew his own face looked no different.

"We all knew this wasn't going to be a fancy-dress ball when we came," he said. "Nobody said this was going to be the easiest way in the world to get rich."

The commander was sitting on one of the carriers, his eyes watching the men, who were lined up in front of him. His voice was purposely held low, but it carried well.

"The marching has been difficult, but now we're really going to see what we're made of.

"We all need a rest, and we all deserve one. But when I lie down to rest, I'm going to do it in a halfway decent bed, with some good, solid food in my belly.

"Here's the way the picture looks: An hour's march from here, there's a good-sized village." He swung partially away from them and pointed south. "I think we have earned that town and every-thing in it."

He swung back, facing them. There was a wolfish grin on his face. "There's gold there, too. Not much, really, compared with what we'll get later on, but enough to whet our appetites."

The men's faces were beginning to change now, in spite of the swelling.

"I don't think we need worry too much about the savages that are living there now. With God on our side, I hardly see how we can fail."

He went on, telling them how they would attack the town, the disposition of men, the use of the carriers, and so forth. By the time he was through, every man there was as eager as he to move in. When he finished speaking, they set up a cheer:

"For the Emperor and the Universal Assembly!"

* * * *

The natives of the small village had heard that some sort of terrible beings were approaching through the jungle. Word had come from the people of the forest that the strange monsters were impervious to darts, and that they had huge dragons with them which were terrifying even to look at. They were clad in metal and made queer noises as they moved.

The village chieftain called his advisers together to ponder the situation. What should they do with these strange things? What were the invaders' intentions?

Obviously, the things must be hostile. Therefore, there were only two courses open—fight or flee. The chieftain and his men decided to fight. It would have been a good thing if there had only been some Imperial troops in the vicinity, but all the troops were farther south, where a civil war was raging over the right of succession of the Greatest Noble.

Nevertheless, there were two thousand fighting men in the village—well, two thousand men at any rate, and they would certainly all fight, although some were rather young and a few were too old for any really hard fighting. On the other hand, it would probably not come to that, since the strangers were outnumbered by at least three to one.

The chieftain gave his orders for the defense of the village.

The invading Earthmen approached the small town cautiously from the west. The commander had his men spread out a little, but not so much that they could be separated. He saw the aliens grouped around the square, boxlike buildings, watching and waiting for trouble.

"We'll give them trouble," the commander whispered softly. He waited until his troops were properly deployed, then he gave the signal for the charge.

The carriers went in first, thundering directly into the massed alien warriors. Each carrier-man fired a single shot from his power weapon, and then went to work with his carrier, running down the terrified aliens, and swinging a sword with one hand while he guided with the other. The commander went in with that first

charge, aiming his own carrier toward the center of the fray. He had some raw, untrained men with him, and he believed in teaching by example.

The aliens recoiled at the onslaught of what they took to be horrible living monsters that were unlike anything ever seen before.

Then the commander's infantry charged in. The shock effect of the carriers had been enough to disorganize the aliens, but the battle was not over yet by a long shot.

There were yells from other parts of the village as some of the other defenders, hearing the sounds of battle, came running to reinforce the home guard. Better than fifteen hundred men were converging on the spot.

The invading Earthmen moved in rapidly against the armed natives, beating them back by the sheer ferocity of their attack. Weapons of steel clashed against weapons of bronze and wood.

The power weapons were used only sparingly; only when the necessity to save a life was greater than the necessity to conserve weapon charges was a shot fired.

The commander, from the center of the fray, took a glance around the area. One glance was enough.

"They're dropping back!" he bellowed, his voice carrying well above the din of the battle, "Keep 'em moving!" He singled out one of his officers at a distance, and yelled: "Hernan! Get a couple of men to cover that street!" He waved toward one of the narrow streets that ran off to one side. The others were already being attended to.

The commander jerked around swiftly as one of the natives grabbed hold of the carrier and tried to hack at the commander with a bronze sword. The commander spitted him neatly on his blade and withdrew it just in time to parry another attack from the other side.

By this time, the reinforcements from the other parts of the village were beginning to come in from the side streets, but they were a little late. The warriors in the square—what was left of them—had panicked. In an effort to get away from the terrible monsters with their deadly blades and their fire-spitting weapons,

they were leaving by the same channels that the reinforcements were coming in by, and the resultant jam-up was disastrous. The panic communicated itself like wildfire, but no one could move fast enough to get away from the sweeping, stabbing, glittering blades of the invading Earthmen.

"All right," the commander yelled, "we've got 'em on the run now! Break up into squads of three and clear those streets! Clear 'em out! Keep 'em moving!"

After that, it was the work of minutes to clear the town.

The commander brought his carrier to a dead stop, reached out with his sword, and snagged a bit of cloth from one of the fallen native warriors. He began to wipe the blade of his weapon as Lieutenant commander Hernan pulled up beside him.

"Casualties?" the commander asked Hernan without looking up from his work.

"Six wounded, no dead," said Hernan. "Or did you want me to count the aliens, too?"

The commander shook his head. "No. Get a detail to clear out the carrion, and then tell Frater Vincent I want to talk to him. We'll have to start teaching these people the Truth."

VIII

"Have you anything to say in your defense?" the commander asked coldly.

For a moment, the accused looked nothing but hatred at the commander, but there was fear behind that hatred. At last he found his voice. "It was mine. You promised us all a share."

Lieutenant commander Hernan picked up a leather bag that lay on the table behind which he and the commander were sitting. With a sudden gesture, he upended it, dumping its contents on the flat, wooden surface of the table.

"Do you deny that this was found among your personal possessions?" he asked harshly.

"No," said the accused soldier. "Why should I? It's mine. Rightfully mine. I fought for it. I found it. I kept it. It's mine." He glanced to either side, towards the two guards who flanked him, then looked back at the commander.

The commander ran an idle finger through the pound or so of golden trinkets that Hernan had spilled from the bag. He knew what the trooper was thinking. A man had a right to what he had earned, didn't he?

The commander picked up one of the heavier bits of primitive jewelry and tossed it in his hand. Then he stood up and looked around the town square.

The company had occupied the town for several weeks. The stored grains in the community warehouse, plus the relaxation the men had had, plus the relative security of the town, had put most of the men back into condition. One had died from a skin infection, and another from wounds sustained in the assault on the town, but the remainder were in good health.

And all of them, with the exception of the sentries guarding the town's perimeter, were standing in the square, watching the court-martial. Their eyes didn't seem to blink, and their breathing was soft and measured. They were waiting for the commander's decision.

The commander, still tossing the crude golden earring, stood

tall and straight, estimating the feeling of the men surrounding him.

"Gold," he said finally. "Gold. That's what we came here for, and that's what we're going to get. Five hundred pounds of the stuff would make any one of you wealthy for the rest of his life. Do you think I blame any one of you for wanting it? Do you think I blame this man here? Of course not." He laughed—a short, hard bark. "Do I blame myself?"

He tossed the bauble again, caught it. "But wanting it is one thing; getting it, holding it, and taking care of it wisely are something else again.

"I gave orders. I have expected—and still expect—that they will be obeyed. But I didn't give them just to hear myself give orders. There was a reason, and a good one.

"Suppose we let each man take what gold he could find. What would happen? The lucky ones would be wealthy, and the unlucky would still be poor. And then some of the lucky ones would wake up some morning without the gold they'd taken because someone else had relieved them of it while they slept.

"And others wouldn't wake up at all, because they'd be found with their throats cut.

"I told you to bring every bit of the metal to me. When this thing is over, every one of you will get his share. If a man dies, his share will be split among the rest, instead of being stolen by someone else or lost because it was hidden too well."

He looked at the earring in his hand, then, with a convulsive sweep of his arm, he tossed it out into the middle of the square.

"There! Seven ounces of gold! Which of you wants it?"

Some of the men eyed the circle of metal that gleamed brightly on the sunlit ground, but none of them made any motion to pick it up.

"So." The commander's voice was almost gentle. He turned his eyes back toward the accused. "You know the orders. You knew them when you hid this." He gestured negligently toward the small heap of native-wrought metal. "Suppose you'd gotten away with it. You'd have ended up with your own share, *plus* this, thereby cheating the others out of—" He glanced at the pile.

"Hm-m-m—say, twenty-five each. And that's only a little compared with what we'll get from now on."

He looked back at the others. "Unless the shares are taken care of *my* way, the largest shares will go to the dishonest, the most powerful, and the luckiest. Unless the division is made as we originally agreed, we'll end up trying to cut each other's heart out."

There was hardness in his voice when he spoke to the accused, but there was compassion there, too.

"First: You have forfeited your share in this expedition. All that you have now, and all that you might have expected will be divided among the others according to our original agreement.

"Second: I do not expect any man to work for nothing. Since you will not receive anything from this expedition, there is no point in your assisting the rest of us or working with us in any way whatsoever.

"Third: We can't have anyone with us who does not carry his own weight."

He glanced at the guards. "Hang him." He paused. "Now."

As he was led away, the commander watched the other men. There was approval in their eyes, but there was something else there, too—a wariness, a concealed fear.

The condemned man turned suddenly and began shouting at the commander, but before he could utter more than three syllables, a fist smashed him down. The guards dragged him off.

"All right, men," said the commander carefully, "let's search the village. There might be more gold about; I have a hunch that this isn't all he hid. Let's see if we can find the rest of it." He sensed the relief of tension as he spoke.

The commander was right. It was amazing how much gold one man had been able to stash away.

IX

They couldn't stay long in any one village; they didn't have the time to sit and relax any more than was necessary. Once they had reached the northern marches of the native empire, it was to the commander's advantage to keep his men moving. He didn't know for sure how good or how rapid communications were among the various native provinces, but he had to assume that they were top notch, allowing for the limitations of a barbaric society.

The worst trouble they ran into on their way was not caused by the native warriors, but by disease.

The route to the south was spotted by great strips of sandy barrenness, torn by winds that swept the grains of sand into the troopers' eyes and crept into the chinks of their armor. Underfoot, the sand made a treacherous pathway; carriers and men alike found it heavy going.

The heat from the sun was intense; the brilliant beams from the primary seemed to penetrate through the men's armor and through the insulation underneath, and made the marching even harder.

Even so, in spite of the discomfort, the men were making good time until the disease struck. And that stopped them in their tracks.

What the disease was or how it was spread is unknown and unknowable at this late date. Virus or bacterium, amoeba or fungus—whatever it was, it struck.

Symptoms: Lassitude, weariness, weakness, and pain.

Signs: Great, ulcerous, wartlike, blood-filled blisters that grew rapidly over the body.

A man might go to sleep at night feeling reasonably tired, but not ill, and wake up in the morning to find himself unable to rise, his muscles too weak to lift him from his bed.

If the blisters broke, or were lanced, it was almost impossible to stop the bleeding, and many died, not from the toxic effect of the disease itself, but from simple loss of blood.

But, like many epidemics, the thing had a fairly short life span. After two weeks, it had burned itself out. Most of those who got it

recovered, and a few were evidently immune.

Eighteen men remained behind in shallow graves.

The rest went on.

X

No man is perfect. Even with four decades of training behind him, Commander Frank couldn't call the turn every time. After the first few villages, there were no further battles. The natives, having seen what the invaders could do, simply showed up missing when the commander and his men arrived. The villages were empty by the time the column reached the outskirts.

Frater Vincent, the agent of the Universal Assembly, complained in no uncertain terms about this state of affairs.

"As you know, commander," he said frowningly one morning, "it's no use trying to indoctrinate a people we can't contact. And you can't subject a people by force of arms alone; the power of the Truth—"

"I know, Frater," the commander interposed quickly. "But we can't deal with these savages in the hinterlands. When we get a little farther into this barbarian empire, we can take the necessary steps to—"

"The Truth," Frater Vincent interrupted somewhat testily, "is for all men. It works, regardless of the state of civilization of the society."

The commander looked out of the unglazed window of the native hut in which he had established his temporary headquarters, in one of the many villages he had taken—or, rather, walked into without a fight because it was empty. "But you'll admit, Frater, that it takes longer with savages."

"True," said Frater Vincent.

"We simply haven't the time. We've got to keep on the move. And, besides, we haven't even been able to contact any of the natives for quite a while; they get out of our way. And we have taken a few prisoners—" His voice was apologetic, but there was a trace of irritation in it. He didn't want to offend Frater Vincent, of course, but dammit, the Assemblyman didn't understand military tactics at all. Or, he corrected himself hastily, at least only slightly.

"Yes," admitted Frater Vincent, "and I've had considerable

success with the prisoners. But, remember—we're not here just to indoctrinate a few occasional prisoners, but to change the entire moral and philosophical viewpoint of an entire race."

"I realize that, Frater," the commander admitted. He turned from the window and faced the Assemblyman. "We're getting close to the Great Bay now. That's where our ship landed on the second probing expedition. I expect we'll be more welcome there than we have been, out here in the countryside. We'll take it easy, and I think you'll have a chance to work with the natives on a mass basis."

The Frater smiled. "Excellent, commander. I . . . uh . . . want you to understand that I'm not trying to tell you your business; you run this campaign as you see fit. But don't lose sight of the ultimate goal of life."

"I won't. How could I? It's just that my methods are not, perhaps, as refined as yours."

Frater Vincent nodded, still smiling. "True. You are a great deal more direct. And—in your own way—just as effective. After all, the Assembly could not function without the military, but there were armies long before the Universal Assembly came into being."

The commander smiled back. "Not any armies like this, Frater."

Frater Vincent nodded. The understanding between the two men—at least on that point—was tacit and mutual. He traced a symbol in the air and left the commander to his thoughts.

Mentally, the commander went through the symbol-patterns that he had learned as a child—the symbol-patterns that brought him into direct contact with the Ultimate Power, the Power that controlled not only the spinning of atoms and the whirling of electrons in their orbits, but the workings of probability itself.

Once indoctrinated into the teachings of the Universal Assembly, any man could tap that Power to a greater or lesser degree, depending on his mental control and ethical attitude. At the top level, a first-class adept could utilize that Power for telepathy, psychokinesis, levitation, teleportation, and other powers that the commander only vaguely understood.

He, himself, had no such depth of mind, such iron control over his will, and he knew he'd never have it. But he could and did tap that Power to the extent that his physical body was under near-perfect control at all times, and not even the fear of death could shake his determination to win or his great courage.

He turned again to the window and looked at the alien sky. There was a great deal yet to be done.

The commander needed information—needed it badly. He had to know what the government of the alien empire was doing. Had they been warned of his arrival? Surely they must have, and yet they had taken no steps to impede his progress.

For this purpose, he decided to set up headquarters on an island just offshore in the Great Bay. It was a protected position, easily defended from assault, and the natives, he knew from his previous visit, were friendly.

They even helped him to get his men and equipment and the carriers across on huge rafts.

From that point, he began collecting the information he needed to invade the central domains of the Greatest Noble himself. It seemed an ideal spot—not only protection-wise, but because this was the spot he had originally picked for the landing of the ship. The vessel, which had returned to the base for reinforcements and extra supplies, would be aiming for the Great Bay area when she came back. And there was little likelihood that atmospheric disturbances would throw her off course again; Captain Bartholomew was too good a man to be fooled twice.

But landing on that island was the first—and only—mistake the commander made during the campaign. The rumors of internal bickerings among the Great Nobles of the barbarian empire were not the only rumors he heard. News of more local treachery came to his ears through the agency of natives, now loyal to the commander, who had been indoctrinated into the philosophy of the Assembly.

A group of native chieftains had decided that the invading Earthmen were too dangerous to be allowed to remain on their

island, in spite of the fact that the invaders had done them no harm. There were, after all, whisperings from the north, whence the invaders had come, that the armored beings with the terrible weapons had used their power more than once during their march to the south. The chieftains were determined to rid their island of the potential menace.

As soon as the matter was brought to the commander's attention, he acted. He sent out a patrol to the place where the ringleaders were meeting, arrested them, and sentenced them to death. He didn't realize what effect that action would have on the rest of the islanders.

He almost found out too late.

XI

"There must be three thousand of them out there," said Lieutenant commander Hernan tightly, "and every one of them's crazy."

"Rot!" The commander spat on the ground and then sighted again along the barrel of his weapon. "I'm the one who's crazy. I'm a lousy politician; that's my trouble."

The lieutenant commander shrugged lightly. "Anyone can make a mistake. Just chalk it up to experience."

"I will, when we get out of this mess." He watched the gathering natives through hard, slitted eyes.

The invading Earthmen were in a village at the southern end of the eight-mile-long island, waiting inside the mud-brick huts while the natives who had surrounded the village worked themselves into a frenzy for an attack. The commander knew there was no sense in charging into them at that point: they would simply scatter and reassemble. The only thing to do was wait until they attacked—and then smash the attack.

"Hernan," he said, his eyes still watching the outside, "you and the others get out there with the carriers after the first volley. Cut them down. They're twenty-to-one against us, so make every blow count. Move."

Hernan nodded wordlessly and slipped away.

The natives were building up their courage with some sort of war dance, whooping and screaming and making threatening gestures toward the embattled invaders. Then the pattern of the dance changed; the islanders whirled to face the mud-brick buildings which housed the invading Earthmen. Suddenly, the dance broke, and the warriors ran in a screaming charge, straight for the trapped soldiers.

The commander waited. His own shot would be the signal, and he didn't want the men to fire too quickly. If the islanders were hit too soon, they might fall back into the woods and set up a siege, which the little company couldn't stand. Better to mop up the natives now, if possible.

Closer. Closer—

Now!

The commander's first shot picked off one of the leaders in the front ranks of the native warriors, and was followed by a raking volley from the other power weapons, firing from the windows of the mud-brick buildings. The warriors in the front rank dropped, and those in the second rank had to move adroitly to keep from stumbling over the bodies of their fallen fellows. The firing from the huts became ragged, but its raking effect was still deadly. A cloud of heavy, stinking smoke rolled across the clearing between the edge of the jungle and the village, as the bright, hard lances of heat leaped from the muzzles of the power weapons toward the bodies of the charging warriors.

The charge was gone from the commander's weapon, and he didn't bother to replace it. As Hernan and his men charged into the melee with their carriers, the commander went with them.

At the same time, the armored infantrymen came pouring out of the mud-brick houses, swinging their swords, straight into the mass of confused native warriors. A picked group of sharpshooters remained behind, in the concealment of the huts to pick off the warriors at the edge of the battle with their sporadic fire.

The commander's lips were moving a little as he formed the symbol-patterns of power almost unconsciously; a lifetime of habit had burned them into his brain so deeply that he could form them automatically while turning the thinking part of his mind to the business at hand.

He soon found himself entirely surrounded by the alien warriors. Their bronze weapons glittered in the sunlight as they tried to fight off the onslaught of the invaders. And those same bronze weapons were sheared, nicked, blunted, bent, and broken as they met the harder steel of the commander's sword.

Then the unexpected happened. One of the warriors, braver than the rest, made a grab for the commander's sword arm. At almost the same moment, a warrior on the other side of the carrier aimed a spear thrust at his side.

Either by itself would have been ineffectual. The spear clanged harmlessly from the commander's armor, and the warrior who had attempted to pull him from the carrier died before he could give

much of a tug. But the combination, plus the fact that the heavy armor was a little unwieldy, overbalanced him. He toppled to the ground with a clash of steel as he and the carrier parted company.

Without a human hand at its controls, the carrier automatically moved away from the mass of struggling fighters and came to a halt well away from the battle.

The commander rolled as he hit and leaped to his feet, his sword moving in flickering arcs around him. The natives had no knowledge of effective swordplay. Like any barbarian, they conceived of a sword as a cutting instrument rather than a thrusting one. They chopped with them, using small shields to protect their bodies as they tried to hack the commander to bits.

But the commander had no desire to become mincemeat just yet. Five of the barbarians were coming at him, their swords raised for a downward slash. The commander lunged forward with a straight stop-thrust aimed at the groin of the nearest one. It came as a complete surprise to the warrior, who doubled up in pain.

The commander had already withdrawn his blade and was attacking the second as the first fell. He made another feint to the groin and then changed the aim of his point as the warrior tried to cover with his shield. A buckler is fine protection against a man who is trying to hack you to death with a chopper, because a heavy cutting sword and a shield have about the same inertia, and thus the same maneuverability. But the shield isn't worth anything against a light stabbing weapon. The warrior's shield started downward and he was unable to stop it and reverse its direction before the commander's sword pierced his throat.

Two down, three to go. No, four. Another warrior had decided to join the little battle against the leader of the invading Earthmen.

The commander changed his tactics just slightly with the third man. He slashed with the tip of his blade against the descending sword-arm of his opponent—a short, quick flick of his wrist that sheared through the inside of the wrist, severing tendons, muscles,

veins and arteries as it cut to the bone. The sword clanged harm-lessly off the commander's shoulder. A quick thrust, and the third man died.

The other three slowed their attack and began circling wari-ly, trying to get behind the commander. Instead of waiting, he charged forward, again cutting at the sword arm of his adversary, severing fingers this time. As the warrior turned, the commander's sword pierced his side.

How long it went on, he had no idea. He kept his legs and his sword-arm moving, and his eyes ever alert for new foes as man after man dropped beneath that snake-tonguing blade. Inside his armor, perspiration poured in rivulets down his skin, and his arms and legs began to ache, but not for one second did he let up. He could not see what was going on, could not tell the direction of the battle nor even allow his mind to wonder what was going on more than ten paces from him.

And then, quite suddenly, it seemed, it was all over. Lieutenant commander Hernan and five other men pulled up with their car-riers, as if from nowhere, their weapons dealing death, clearing a space around their commander.

"You hurt?" bawled Hernan.

The commander paused to catch his breath. He knew there was a sword-slash across his face, and his right leg felt as though there was a cut on it, but otherwise—

"I'm all right," he said. "How's it going?"

"They're breaking," Hernan told him. "We'll have them scat-tered within minutes."

Even as he spoke, the surge of battle moved away from them, toward the forest. The charge of the carriers, wreaking havoc on every side, had broken up the battle formation the aliens had had; the flaming death from the horrible weapons of the invaders, the fearless courage of the foot soldiers, and the steel-clad monsters that were running amuck among them shattered the little disci-pline they had. Panicky, they lost their anger, which had taken them several hours to build up. They scattered, heading for the forest.

Shortly, the village was silent. Not an alien warrior was to be

seen, save for the hundreds of mute corpses that testified to the carnage that had been wrought.

Several of the commander's men had been wounded, and three had died. Lieutenant commander Hernan had been severely wounded in the leg by a native javelin, but the injury was a long way from being fatal.

Hernan gritted his teeth while his leg was being bandaged. "The angels were with us on that one," he said between winces.

The commander nodded. "I hope they stick with us. We'll need 'em to get off this island."

XII

For a while, it looked as though they were trapped on the island. The natives didn't dare to attack again, but no hunting party was safe, and the food supply was dropping. They had gotten on the island only by the help of the natives, who had ferried them over on rafts. But getting off was another thing, now that the natives were hostile. Cutting down trees to build rafts might possibly be managed, but during the loading the little company would be too vulnerable to attack.

The commander was seated bleakly in the hut he had taken as his headquarters, trying to devise a scheme for getting to the mainland, when the deadlock was finally broken.

There was a flurry of footsteps outside, a thump of heavy boots as one of the younger officers burst into the room.

"Commander!" he yelled. "Commander! Come outside!"

The commander leaped to his feet. "Another attack?"

"No, sir! Come look!"

The commander strode quickly to the door. His sight followed the line of the young officer's pointing finger.

There, outlined against the blue of the sky, was a ship!

The news from home was encouraging, but it was a long way from being what the commander wanted. Another hundred men and more carriers had been added to the original company of now hardened veterans, and the recruits, plus the protection of the ship's guns, were enough to enable the entire party to leave the island for the mainland.

By this time, the commander had gleaned enough information from the natives to be able to plan the next step in his campaign. The present Greatest Noble, having successfully usurped the throne from his predecessor, was still not in absolute control of the country. He had won a civil war, but his rule was still too shaky to allow him to split up his armies, which accounted for the fact that, thus far, no action had been taken by the Imperial

troops against the invading Earthmen.

The commander set up a base on the mainland, near the coast, left a portion of his men there to defend it, and, with the remainder, marched inland to come to grips with the Greatest Noble himself.

As they moved in toward the heart of the barbarian empire, the men noticed a definite change in the degree of civilization of the natives—or, at least, in the degree of technological advancement. There were large towns, not small villages, to be dealt with, and there were highways and bridges that showed a knowledge of engineering equivalent to that of ancient Rome.

The engineers of the Empire of the Great Nobles were a long way above the primitive. They could have, had they had any reason to, erected a pyramid the equal of great Khufu's in size, and probably even more neatly constructed. Militarily speaking, the lack of knowledge of iron hampered them, but it must be kept in mind that a well-disciplined and reasonably large army, armed with bronze-tipped spears, bronze swords, axes, and maces, can make a formidable foe, even against a much better equipped group.

The Imperial armies were much better disciplined and much better armed than any of the natives the commander had thus far dealt with, and there were reputed to be more than ten thousand of them with the Greatest Noble in his mountain stronghold. Such considerations prompted the commander to plan his strategy carefully, but they did not deter him in the least. If he had been able to bring aircraft and perhaps a thermonuclear bomb or two for demonstration purposes, the attack might have been less risky, but neither had been available to a man of his limited means, so he had to work without them.

But now, he avoided fighting if at all possible. Working with Frater Vincent, the commander worked to convince the natives on the fertile farms and in the prosperous villages that he and his company were merely ambassadors of good will—missionaries and traders. He and his men had come in peace, and if they were received in peace, well and good. If not . . . well, they still had their weapons.

The commander was depending on the vagueness of the information that may have filtered down from the north. The news had already come that the invaders were fierce and powerful fighters, but the commander gave the impression that the only reason any battles had taken place was because the northern tribes had been truculent in the extreme. He succeeded fairly well; the natives he now met considered their brethren of the northern provinces to be little better than savages, and therefore to be expected to treat strangers inhospitably and bring about their own ruin. The southern citizens of the empire eyed the strangers with apprehension, but they offered very little resistance. The commander and his men were welcomed warily at each town, and, when they left, were bid farewell with great relief.

It took a little time for the commander to locate the exact spot where the Greatest Noble and his retinue were encamped. The real capital of the empire was located even farther south, but the Greatest Noble was staying, for the nonce, in a city nestled high in the mountains, well inland from the seacoast. The commander headed for the mountains.

The passage into the mountains wasn't easy. The passes were narrow and dangerous, and the weather was cold. The air became thinner at every step. At eight thousand feet, mountain climbing in heavy armor becomes more than just hard work, and at twelve thousand it becomes exhausting torture. But the little company went on, sparked, fueled, and driven by the personal force of their commander, who stayed in the vanguard, his eyes ever alert for treachery from the surrounding mountains.

When the surprise came, it was of an entirely different kind than he had expected. The commander's carrier came over a little rise, and he brought it to an abrupt halt as he saw the valley spread out beneath him. He left the carrier, walked over to a boulder near the edge of the cliff, and looked down at the valley.

It was an elongated oval of verdant green, fifteen miles long by four wide, looking like an emerald set in the rocky granite of the surrounding peaks that thrust upward toward the sky. The valley ran roughly north-and-south, and to his right, at the

southern end, the commander could see a city, although it was impossible to see anyone moving in it at this distance.

To his left, he could see great clouds of billowing vapor that rolled across the grassy plain—evidently steam from the volcanic hot springs which he had been told were to be found in this valley.

But, for the moment, it was neither the springs nor the city that interested him most.

In the heart of the valley, spreading over acre after acre, were the tents and pavilions of a mighty army encampment. From the looks of it, the estimate of thirty thousand troops which had been given him by various officials along the way was, if anything, too small.

It was a moment that might have made an ordinary man stop to think, and, having thought, to turn and go. But the commander was no ordinary man, and the sheer remorseless courage that had brought him this far wouldn't allow him to turn back. So far, he had kept the Greatest Noble off balance with his advancing tactics; if he started to retreat, the Greatest Noble would realize that the invaders were not invincible, and would himself advance to crush the small band of strangers.

The Greatest Noble had known the commander and his men were coming; he was simply waiting, to find out what they were up to, confident that he could dispose of them at his leisure. The commander knew that, and he knew he couldn't retreat now. There was no decision to be made, really—only planning to be done.

He turned back from the boulder to face the officers who had come to take a look at the valley.

"We'll go to the city first," he said.

XIII

The heavy tread of the invaders' boots as they entered the central plaza of the walled city awakened nothing but echoes from the stone walls that surrounded the plaza. Like the small villages they had entered farther north, the city seemed devoid of life.

There is nothing quite so depressing and threatening as a deserted city. The windows in the walls of the buildings seemed like blank, darkened eyes that watched—and waited. Nothing moved, nothing made a sound, except the troopers themselves.

The men kept close to the walls; there was no point in bunching up in the middle of the square to be cut down by arrows from the windows of the upper floors.

The commander ordered four squads of men to search the buildings and smoke out anyone who was there, but they turned up nothing. The entire city was empty. And there were no traps, no ambushes—nothing.

The commander, with Lieutenant commander Hernan and another officer, climbed to the top of the central building of the town. In the distance, several miles away, they could see the encampment of the monarch's troops.

"The only thing we can do," the commander said, his face hard and determined, "is to call their bluff. You two take about three dozen men and go out there with the carriers and give them a show. Go right into camp, as if you owned the place. Throw a scare into them, but don't hurt anyone. Then, very politely, tell the Emperor, or whatever he calls himself, that I would like him to come here for dinner and a little talk."

The two officers looked at each other, then at the commander.

"Just like that?" asked Hernan.

"Just like that," said the commander.

The demonstration and exhibition went well—as far as it had gone. The native warriors had evidently been quite impressed by the onslaught of the terrifying monsters that had thundered across

the plain toward them, right into the great camp, and come to a dead halt directly in front of the magnificent pavilion of the Greatest Noble himself.

The Greatest Noble put up a good face. He had obviously been expecting the visitors, because he and his lesser nobles were lined up before the pavilion, the Greatest Noble ensconced on a sort of portable throne. He managed to look perfectly calm and somewhat bored by the whole affair, and didn't seem to be particularly effected at all when Lieutenant commander Hernan bowed low before him and requested his presence in the city.

And the Greatest Noble's answer was simple and to the point, although it was delivered by one of his courtiers.

"You may tell your commander," said the noble, "that His Effulgence must attend to certain religious duties tonight, since he is also High Priest of the Sun. However, His Effulgence will most graciously deign to speak to your commander tomorrow. In the meantime, you are requested to enjoy His Effulgence's gracious hospitality in the city, which has been emptied for your convenience. It is yours, for the nonce."

Which left nothing for the two officers and their men to do but go thundering back across the plain to the city.

The Greatest Noble did not bring his whole army with him, but the pageant of barbaric splendor that came tootling and drumming its way into the city the next evening was a magnificent sight. His Effulgence himself was dressed in a scarlet robe and a scarlet, turbanlike head covering with scarlet fringes all around it. About his throat was a necklace of emerald-green gems, and his clothing was studded with more of them. Gold gleamed everywhere. He was borne on an ornate, gilded palanquin, carried high above the crowd on the shoulders of a dozen stalwart nobles, only slightly less gorgeously-dressed than the Greatest Noble. The nobility that followed was scarcely less showy in its finery.

When they came into the plaza, however, the members of the procession came to a halt. The singing and music died away.

The plaza was absolutely empty.

No one had come out to greet the Emperor.

There were six thousand natives in the plaza, and not a sign of the invaders.

The commander, hiding well back in the shadows in one of the rooms of the central building, watched through the window and noted the evident consternation of the royal entourage with satisfaction. Frater Vincent, standing beside him, whispered, "Well?"

"All right," the commander said softly, "they've had a taste of what we got when we came in. I suppose they've had enough. Let's go out and act like hosts."

The commander and a squad of ten men, along with Frater Vincent, strode majestically out of the door of the building and walked toward the Greatest Noble. They had all polished their armor until it shone, which was about all they could do in the way of finery, but they evidently looked quite impressive in the eyes of the natives.

"Greetings, Your Effulgence," said the commander, giving the Greatest Noble a bow that was hardly five degrees from the perpendicular. "I trust we find you well."

In the buildings surrounding the square, hardly daring to move for fear the clank of metal on metal might give the whole plan away, the remaining members of the company watched the conversation between their commander and the Greatest Noble. They couldn't hear what was being said, but that didn't matter; they knew what to do as soon as the commander gave the signal. Every eye was riveted on the commander's right hand.

It seemed an eternity before the commander casually reached up to his helmet and brushed a hand across it—once—twice—three times.

Then all hell broke loose. The air was split by the sound of power weapons throwing their lances of flame into the massed ranks of the native warriors. The gunners, safe behind the walls of the buildings, poured a steady stream of accurately directed fire into the packed mob, while the rest of the men charged in with their blades, thrusting and slashing as they went.

The aliens, panic-stricken by the sudden, terrifying assault, tried to run, but there was nowhere to run to. Every exit had been cut off to bottle up the Imperial cortege. Within minutes, the entrances to the square were choked with the bodies of those who tried to flee.

As soon as the firing began, the commander and his men began to make their way toward the Greatest Noble. They had been forced to stand a good five yards away during the parlay, cut off from direct contact by the Imperial guards. The commander, sword in hand, began cutting his way through to the palanquin.

The palanquin bearers seemed frozen; they couldn't run, they couldn't fight, and they didn't dare drop their precious cargo.

The commander's voice bellowed out over the carnage. "Take him prisoner! I'll personally strangle the idiot who harms him!" And then he was too busy to yell.

Two members of the Greatest Noble's personal guard came for him, swords out, determined to give their lives, if necessary, to preserve the sacred life of their monarch. And give them they did.

The commander's blade lashed out once, sliding between the ribs of the first guard. He toppled and almost took the sword with him, but the commander wrenched it free in time to parry the downward slash of the second guard's bronze sword. It was a narrow thing, because the bronze sword, though of softer stuff than the commander's steel, was also heavier, and thus hard to deflect. As it sang past him, the commander swung a chop at the man's neck, cutting it halfway through. He stepped quickly to one side to avoid the falling body and thrust his blade through a third man, who was aiming a blow at the neck of one of the commander's officers. There were only a dozen feet separating the commander from his objective, the palanquin of the Greatest Noble, but he had to wade through blood to get there.

The palanquin itself was no longer steady. Three of the twelve nobles who had been holding it had already fallen, and there were two of the commander's men already close enough to touch the

royal person, but they were too busy fighting to make any attempt to grab him. The Greatest Noble, unarmed, could only huddle in his seat, terrified, but it would take more than two men to snatch him from his bodyguard. The commander fought his way in closer.

Two more of the palanquin bearers went down, and the palanquin itself began to topple. The Greatest Noble screamed as he fell toward the commander.

One of the commander's men spun around as he heard the scream so close to him, and, thinking that the Greatest Noble was attacking his commander, lunged out with his blade.

It was almost a disaster. Moving quickly, the commander threw out his left arm to deflect the sword. He succeeded, but he got a bad slash across his hand for his trouble.

He yelled angrily at the surprised soldier, not caring what he said. Meanwhile, the others of the squad, seeing that the Greatest Noble had fallen, hurried to surround him. Two minutes later, the Greatest Noble was a prisoner, being half carried, half led into the central building by four of the men, while the remaining six fought a rear-guard action to hold off the native warriors who were trying to rescue the sacred person of the Child of the Sun.

Once inside, the Greatest Noble was held fast while the doors were swung shut.

Outside, the slaughter went on. All the resistance seemed to go out of the warriors when they saw their sacred monarch dragged away by the invading Earthmen. It was every man for himself and the Devil take the hindmost. And the Devil, in the form of the commander's troops, certainly did.

Within half an hour after it had begun, the butchery was over. More than three thousand of the natives had died, and an unknown number more badly wounded. Those who had managed to get out and get away from the city kept on going. They told the troops who had been left outside what had happened, and a mass exodus from the valley began.

Safely within the fortifications of the central building, the commander allowed himself one of his rare grins of satisfaction. Not a single one of his own men had been killed, and the only wound

which had been sustained by anyone in the company was the cut on his own hand. Still smiling, he went into the room where the Greatest Noble, dazed and shaken, was being held by two of the commander's men. The commander bowed—this time, very low.

"I believe, Your Effulgence, that we have an appointment for dinner. Come, the banquet has been laid."

And, as though he were still playing the gracious host, the commander led the half-paralyzed Child of the Sun to the room where the banquet had been put on a table in perfect diplomatic array.

"Your Effulgence may sit at my right hand," said the commander pleasantly.

XIV

As MacDonald said of Robert Wilson, "This is not an account of how Boosterism came to Arcadia." It's a devil of a long way from it. And once the high point of a story has been reached and passed, it is pointless to prolong it too much. The capture of the Greatest Noble broke the power of the Empire of the Great Nobles forever. The loyal subjects were helpless without a leader, and the disloyal ones, near the periphery of the Empire, didn't care. The crack Imperial troops simply folded up and went home. The Greatest Noble went on issuing orders, and they were obeyed; the people were too used to taking orders from authority to care whether they were really the Greatest Noble's own idea or not.

In a matter of months, two hundred men had conquered an empire, with a loss of thirty-five or forty men. Eventually, they had to execute the old Greatest Noble and put his more tractable nephew on the throne, but that was a mere incident.

Gold? It flowed as though there were an endless supply. The commander shipped enough back on the first load to make them all wealthy.

The commander didn't go back home to spend his wealth amid the luxuries of the Imperial court, even though Emperor Carl appointed him to the nobility. That sort of thing wasn't the commander's meat. There, he would be a fourth-rate noble; here, he was the Imperial Viceroy, responsible only to the distant Emperor. There, he would be nothing; here, he was almost a king.

Two years after the capture of the Greatest Noble, he established a new capital on the coast and named it Kingston. And from Kingston he ruled with an iron hand.

As has been intimated, this was *not* Arcadia. A year after the founding of Kingston, the old capital was attacked, burned, and almost fell under siege, due to a sudden uprising of the natives under the new Greatest Noble, who had managed to escape. But the uprising collapsed because of the approach of the planting season; the warriors had to go back home and plant their crops or

the whole of the agriculture-based country would starve—except the invading Earthmen.

Except in a few instances, the natives were never again any trouble.

But the commander—now the Viceroy—had not seen the end of his troubles.

He had known his limitations, and realized that the governing of a whole planet—or even one continent—was too much for one man when the population consists primarily of barbarians and savages. So he had delegated the rule of a vast area to the south to another—a Lieutenant commander James, known as "One-Eye," a man who had helped finance the original expedition, and had arrived after the conquest.

One-Eye went south and made very small headway against the more barbaric tribes there. He did not become rich, and he did not achieve anywhere near the success that the Viceroy had. So he came back north with his army and decided to unseat the Viceroy and take his place. That was five years after the capture of the Greatest Noble.

One-Eye took Center City, the old capital, and started to work his way northward, toward Kingston. The Viceroy's forces met him at a place known as Salt Flats and thoroughly trounced him. He was captured, tried for high treason, and executed.

One would think that the execution ended the threat of Lieutenant commander James, but not so. He had a son, and he had had followers.

XV

Nine years. Nine years since the breaking of a vast empire. It really didn't seem like it. The Viceroy looked at his hands. They were veined and thin, and the callouses were gone. Was he getting soft, or just getting old? A little bit—no, a *great deal* of both.

He sat in his study, in the Viceregal Palace at Kingston, chewing over the events of the past weeks. Twice, rumors had come that he was to be assassinated. He and two of his councilors had been hanged in effigy in the public square not long back. He had been snubbed publicly by some of the lesser nobles.

Had he ruled harshly, or was it just jealousy? And was it, really, as some said, caused by the Southerners and the followers of Young Jim?

He didn't know. And sometimes, it seemed as if it didn't matter.

Here he was, sitting alone in his study, when he should have gone to a public function. And he had stayed because of fear of assassination.

Was it—

There was a knock at the door.

"Come in."

A servant entered. "Sir Martin is here, my lord."

The Viceroy got to his feet. "Show him in, by all means."

Sir Martin, just behind the servant, stepped in, smiling, and the Viceroy returned his smile. "Well, everything went off well enough without you," said Sir Martin.

"Any sign of trouble?"

"None, my lord; none whatsoever. The—"

"Damn!" the Viceroy interrupted savagely. "I should have known! What have I done but display my cowardice? I'm getting yellow in my old age!"

Sir Martin shook his head. "Cowardice, my lord? Nothing of the sort. Prudence, I should call it. By the by, the judge and a few others are coming over." He chuckled softly. "We thought we might talk you out of a meal."

The Viceroy grinned widely. "Nothing easier. I suspected all you hangers-on would come around for your handouts. Come along, my friend; we'll have a drink before the others get here."

There were nearly twenty people at dinner, all, presumably, friends of the Viceroy. At least, it is certain that they were friends in so far as they had no part in the assassination plot. It was a gay party; the Viceroy's friends were doing their best to cheer him up, and were succeeding pretty well. One of the nobles, known for his wit, had just essayed a somewhat off-color jest, and the others were roaring with laughter at the punch line when a shout rang out.

There was a sudden silence around the table.

"What was that?" asked someone. "What did—"

"*Help!*" There was the sound of footsteps pounding up the stairway from the lower floor.

"*Help! The Southerners have come to kill the Viceroy!*"

From the sounds, there was no doubt in any of the minds of the people seated around the table that the shout was true. For a moment, there was shock. Then panic took over.

There were only a dozen or so men in the attacking party; if the "friends" of the Viceroy had stuck by him, they could have held off the assassins with ease.

But no one ran to lock the doors that stood between the Viceroy and his enemies, and only a few drew their weapons to defend him. The others fled. Getting out of a window from the second floor of a building isn't easy, but fear can lend wings, and, although none of them actually flew down, the retreat went fast enough.

Characteristically, the Viceroy headed, not for the window, but for his own room, where his armor—long unused, except for state functions—hung waiting in the closet. With him went Sir Martin.

But there wasn't even an opportunity to get into the armor. The rebel band charged into the hallway that led to the bedroom, screaming: "*Death to the Tyrant! Long live the Emperor!*"

It was personal anger, then, not rebellion against the Empire which had appointed the ex-commander to his post as Viceroy.

"Where is the Viceroy? Death to the Tyrant!" The assassins moved in.

Swords in hand, and cloaks wrapped around their left arms, Sir Martin and the Viceroy moved to meet the oncoming attackers.

"Traitors!" bellowed the Viceroy. "Cowards! Have you come to kill me in my own house?"

Parry, thrust! Parry, thrust! Two of the attackers fell before the snake-tongue blade of the fighting Viceroy. Sir Martin accounted for two more before he fell in a flood of his own blood.

The Viceroy was alone, now. His blade flickered as though inspired, and two more died under its tireless onslaught. Even more would have died if the head of the conspiracy, a supporter of Young Jim named Rada, hadn't pulled a trick that not even the Viceroy would have pulled.

Rada grabbed one of his own men and shoved him toward the Viceroy's sword, impaling the hapless man upon that deadly blade.

And, in the moment while the Viceroy's weapon was buried to the hilt in an enemy's body, the others leaped around the dying man and ran their blades through the Viceroy.

He dropped to the floor, blood gushing from half a dozen wounds.

Even so, his fighting heart still had seconds more to beat. As he propped himself up on one arm, the assassins stood back; even they recognized that they had killed something bigger and stronger than they. A better man than any of them lay dying at their feet.

He clawed with one hand at the river of red that flowed from his pierced throat and then fell forward across the stone floor. With his crimson hand, he traced the great symbol of his Faith on the stone—the Sign of the Cross. He bent his head to kiss it, and, with a final cry of "*Jesus!*" he died. At the age of seventy, it had taken a dozen men to kill him with treachery, something all the hell of nine years of conquest and rule had been unable to do.

And thus died Francisco Pizarro, the Conqueror of Peru.

THE END

To be read after you have finished
"Despoilers of the Golden Empire."

Dear John,

It has been brought to my attention, by those who have read the story, that "Despoilers of the Golden Empire" might conceivably be charged with being a "reader cheater"—*i.e.*, that it does not play fair with the reader, but leads him astray by means of false statements. Naturally, I feel it me bounden duty to refute such scurrilous and untrue affronts, and thus save meself from opprobrium.

Therefore, I address what follows to the interested reader:

It cannot be denied that you must have been misled when you read the story; indeed, I'd be the last to deny it, since I *intended* that you should be misled. What I most certainly *do* deny is any implication that such misleading was accomplished by the telling of untruths. A fiction writer is, *by definition*, a professional liar; he makes his living by telling interesting lies on paper and selling the results to the highest bidder for publication. Since fiction writing is my livelihood, I cannot and will not deny that I am an accomplished liar—indeed, almost an habitual one. Therefore, I feel some small pique when, on the one occasion on which I stick strictly to the truth, I am accused of fraud. *Pfui!* say I; I refute you. "I deny the allegation, and I defy the alligator!"

To prove my case, I shall take several examples from "Despoilers" and show that the statements made are perfectly valid. (Please note that I do not claim any absolute accuracy for such details as quoted dialogue, except that none of the characters lies. I simply contend that the story is as accurate as any other good historical novelette. I also might say here that any resemblance between "Despoilers" and any story picked at random from the late lamented *Planet Stories* is purely intentional and carefully contrived.)

Take the first sentence:

"In the seven centuries that had elapsed since the Second Empire had been founded on the shattered remnants of the First, the

nobles of the Imperium had come slowly to realize that the empire was not to be judged by the examples of its predecessor."

Perfectly true. By the time of the Renaissance, the nobles of the Holy Roman Empire knew that their empire was not just a continuation of the Roman Empire, but a new entity. The old Roman Empire had collapsed in the Sixth Century, and the *Holy* Roman Empire, which was actually a loose confederation of Germanic states, did not come into being until A. D. 800, when Karl der Grosse (Charlemagne) was crowned emperor by the Pope.

Anyone who wishes to quibble that the date should be postponed for a century and a half, until the time of the German prince, Otto, may do so; I will ignore him.

A few paragraphs later, I said:

"Without power, neither Civilization nor the Empire could hold itself together, and His Universal Majesty, the Emperor Carl, well knew it. And power was linked solidly to one element, one metal . . ."

The metal, as I said later on, was Gold-197.

By "power," of course, I meant political and economic power. In the Sixteenth Century, that's what almost anyone would have meant. If you chose to interpret it as meaning "energy per unit time," why, that's real tough.

Why nail the "power metal" down to an isotope of gold with an atomic weight of 197? Because that's the only naturally occurring isotope of gold.

The "Emperor Carl" was, of course, Charles V, who also happened to be King of Spain, and therefore Pizarro's sovereign. I Germanicized his name, as I did the others—Francisco Pizarro becomes "Frank," et cetera—but this is perfectly legitimate. After all, the king's name in Latin, which was used in all state papers, was *Carolus*; the Spanish called him *Carlos*, and history books in English call him *Charles*. Either *Karl* or *Carl* is just as legitimate as *Charles*, certainly, and the same applies to the other names in the story.

As to the title "His Universal Majesty," that's exactly what

he *was* called. It is usually translated as "His Catholic Majesty," but the word *Catholic* comes from the Greek *katholikos*, meaning "universal." And, further on in the story, when the term "Universal Assembly" is used, it is a direct translation of the Greek term, *Ekklesia Katholikos*, and is actually a better translation than "Catholic Church," since the English word *church* comes from the Greek *kyriakon*, meaning "the house of the Lord"—in other words, a church *building*, not the organization as a whole.

Toward the end of Chapter One, I wrote:

> "Throughout the Empire, research laboratories worked tirelessly at the problem of transmuting commoner elements into Gold-197, but thus far none of the processes was commercially feasible."

I think you will admit that the alchemists never found a method of transmuting the elements—certainly none which was commercially feasible.

In Chapter Three, the statement that Pizarro left his home—Spain—with undermanned ships, and had to sneak off illegally before the King's inspectors checked up on him, is historically accurate. And who can argue with the statement that "there wasn't a scientist worthy of the name in the whole outfit"?

At the beginning of Chapter Four, you'll find:

> "Due to atmospheric disturbances, the ship's landing was several hundred miles from the point the commander had originally picked . . ." and ". . . the ship simply wasn't built for atmospheric navigation."

The adverse winds which drove Pizarro's ships off course were certainly "atmospheric disturbances," and I defy anyone to prove that a Sixteenth Century Spanish galleon was built for atmospheric navigation.

And I insist that using the term "carrier" instead of "horse," while misleading, is not inaccurate. However, I *would* like to know just what sort of picture the term conjured up in the reader's mind. In Chapter Ten, in the battle scene, you'll find the following:

"The combination [of attackers from both sides], plus the fact that the heavy armor was a little unwieldy, overbalanced him [the commander]. He toppled to the ground with a clash of steel as he and the carrier parted company.

"Without a human hand at its controls, the carrier automatically moved away from the mass of struggling fighters and came to a halt well away from the battle."

To be perfectly honest, it's somewhat of a strain on my mind to imagine anyone building a robot-controlled machine as good as all that, and then giving the drive such poor protection that he can fall off of it.

One of the great screams from my critics has been occasioned by the fact that I referred several times to the Spaniards as "Earthmen." I can't see why. In order not to confuse the reader, I invariably referred to them as the "*invading* Earthmen," so as to make a clear distinction between them and the *native* Earthmen, or Incas, who were native to Peru. If this be treachery, then make the most of it.

In other words, I contend that I simply did what any other good detective story writer tries to do—mislead the reader without lying to him. Agatha Christie's "The Murder of Roger Ackroyd," for instance, uses the device of telling the story from the murderer's viewpoint, in the first person, without revealing that he *is* the murderer. Likewise, John Dickson Carr, in his "Nine Wrong Answers" finds himself forced to deny that he has lied to the reader, although he admits that one of his characters certainly lied. Both Carr and Christie told the absolute truth—within the framework of the story—and left it to the reader to delude himself.

It all depends on the viewpoint. The statement, "We all liked Father Goodheart very much" means one thing when said by a member of his old parish in the United States, which he left to become a missionary. It means something else again when uttered by a member of the tribe of cannibals which the good Father attempted unsuccessfully to convert.

Similarly, such terms as "the gulf between the worlds," "the new world," and "the known universe" have one meaning to a

science-fictioneer, and another to a historian. Semantics, anyone?

In Chapter Ten, right at the beginning, there is a conversation between Commander Frank and Frater Vincent, and "agent of the Assembly" (read: *priest*). If the reader will go back over that section, keeping in mind the fact that what they are "actually" talking about are the Catholic Church and the Christian religion *as seen from the viewpoint of a couple of fanatically devout Sixteenth Century Spaniards*, he will understand the method I used in presenting the whole story.

Let me quote:

> "Mentally, the commander went through the symbol-patterns that he had learned as a child—the symbol-patterns that brought him into direct contact with the Ultimate Power, the Power that controlled not only the spinning of atoms and the whirling of electrons in their orbits, but the workings of probability itself."

Obviously, he is reciting the *Pater Noster* and the *Ave Maria*. The rest of the sentence is self-explanatory.

So is the following:

> "Once indoctrinated into the teachings of the Universal Assembly, any man could tap that power to a greater or lesser degree, depending on his mental control and ethical attitude. At the top level, a first-class adept could utilize that Power for telepathy, psychokinesis, levitation, teleportation, and other powers that the commander only vaguely understood."

It doesn't matter whether *you* believe in the miracles attributed to many of the Saints; Pizarro certainly did. His faith in that Power was as certain as the modern faith in the power of the atomic bomb.

As a matter of fact, it was very probably that hard, unyielding Faith which made the Sixteenth Century Spaniard the almost superhuman being that he was. Only Spain of the Sixteenth Century could have produced the Conquistadors or such a man as St. Ignatius Loyola, whose learned, devout, and fanatically militant Society of Jesus struck fear into the hearts of Protestant and Catholic

Princes alike for the next two centuries.

The regular reader of *Astounding* may remember that I gave another example of the technique of truthful misdirection in "The Best Policy," (July, 1957). An Earthman, captured by aliens, finds himself in a position in which he is unable to tell even the smallest lie. But by telling the absolute truth, he convinces the aliens that *homo sapiens* is a race of super-duper supermen. He does it so well that the aliens surrender without attacking, even before the rest of humanity is aware of their existence.

The facts in "Despoilers of the Golden Empire" remain. They *are* facts. Francisco Pizarro and his men—an army of less than two hundred—actually *did* inflict appalling damage on the Inca armies, even if they were outnumbered ten to one, and with astonishingly few losses of their own. They did it with sheer guts, too; their equipment was not too greatly superior to that of the Peruvians, and by the time they reached the Great Inca himself, none of the Peruvians believed that the invaders were demons or gods. But in the face of the Spaniards' determined onslaught, they were powerless.

The assassination scene at the end is almost an exact description of what happened. It *did* take a dozen men in full armor to kill the armorless Pizarro, and even then it took trickery and treachery to do it.

Now, just to show how fair I was—to show how I scrupulously refrained from lying—I will show what a sacrifice I made for the sake of truth.

If you'll recall, in the story, the dying Pizarro traces the Sign of the Cross on the floor in his own blood, kisses it, and says "*Jesus!*" before he dies. This is in strict accord with every history on the subject I could find.

But there is a legend to the effect that his last words were somewhat different. I searched the New York Public Library for days trying to find one single historian who would bear out the legend; I even went so far as to get a librarian who could read Spanish and another whose German is somewhat better than mine to translate articles in foreign historical journals for me. All in vain. But if I *could* have substantiated the legend, the final scene would have

read something like this:

> Clawing at his sword-torn throat, the fearless old soldier brought his hand away coated with the crimson of his own blood. Falling forward, he traced the Sign of the Cross on the stone floor in gleaming scarlet, kissed it, and then glared up at the men who surrounded him, his eyes hard with anger and hate.

"I'm going to Heaven," he said, his voice harsh and whispery. "And *you*, you *bastards*, can go to *Hell*!"

It would have made one hell of an ending—but it had to be sacrificed in the interests of Truth.

So I rest my case.

I will even go further than that; I defy anyone to point out a single out-and-out lie in the whole story. G'wan—I *dare* ya!

(SECRET ASIDE TO THE READER;
J. W. C., Jr.,[1] PLEASE DO NOT READ!)

Ah, but wait! There *is* a villain in the piece!

I did not lie to you, no. But you were lied to, all the same.

By whom?

By none less than that conniving arch-fiend, John W. Campbell, Jr., that's who!

Wasn't it he who bought the story?

And wasn't it he who, with malice aforethought, published it in a package which was plainly labeled Science Fiction?

And, therefore, didn't you have every right to think it *was* science fiction?

Sure you did!

I am guilty of nothing more than weakness; my poor, frail sense of ethics collapsed completely at the sight of the bribe he offered me to become a party to the dark conspiracy that sprang from the depths of his own demoniac mind. Ah, well; none of us is perfect, I suppose.

---

1   John W. Campbell, Jr., editor of *Astounding Science Fiction*, published this story. (It's probably safe to say he read the secret aside!) —JGB

ABOUT THE AUTHOR

Randall Garrett (1927-1987) was an American science fiction and fantasy author. He was a prolific contributor to *Astounding* and other science fiction magazines of the 1950s and 1960s. He instructed Robert Silverberg in the techniques of selling large quantities of action-adventure science fiction, and collaborated with him on two novels about Earth bringing civilization to an alien planet.

Garrett is best known for the Lord Darcy books, the novel *Too Many Magicians* and two short story collections, set in an alternate world where a joint Anglo-French empire still led by a Plantagenet dynasty has survived into the twentieth century and where magic works and has been scientifically codified. The Darcy books are rich in jokes, puns, and references (particularly to works of detective and spy fiction: Lord Darcy is himself partially modelled on Sherlock Holmes), elements that often appear in the shorter works about the detective. Michael Kurland wrote two additional Lord Darcy novels.

Garrett wrote under a variety of pseudonyms including: David Gordon, John Gordon, Darrel T. Langart (an anagram of his name), Alexander Blade, Richard Greer, Ivar Jorgensen, Clyde Mitchell, Leonard G. Spencer, S. M. Tenneshaw, Gerald Vance. He was also a founding member of the Society for Creative Anachronism, as "Randall of Hightower" (a pun on "garret"). The short novel *Brain Twister*, written by Garrett in conjunction with author Laurence Janifer (using the joint pseudonym Mark Phillips) was nominated for the Hugo Award for Best Novel in 1960.

An inveterate punster (defining a pun as "the odor given off by a decaying mind"), he was a favorite guest at science fiction conventions and friend to many fans, especially in Southern California.